* * * *

Stairs to you

Copyright © 2017 by Christy Dilg

Paperback Edition

Printed in the United States of America

First Edition: June 2017

Library of Congress Cataloging-in-Publication Data

Dilg, Christy

Stairs to you – 1st ed

ISBN-13: 978-1547144532
ISBN-10: 154714453X

* * *

Letter to my Readers:

This book idea began because of the loss and complete deviation of losing my dad to colon cancer. I wanted to write something that would reflect my love for him and his love for his wife. I didn't want to write a story where the man was a jerk or man-whore, but instead a about a man that truly loved one woman with everything he had. So many people told me Dare was a wimp and he needed to move on with his life, but I knew from watching my dad love his wife with his whole heart, that true love exists. That a one-woman man is out there.

Once I began writing the story of Atlanta and Dare my sister got very sick. Our family watched her battle endocarditis that began from a pulled tooth that got an infection that spread into her blood stream, and caused severe damage to her heart. After three open heart surgeries, two procedures, and multiple problems she ended up losing her battle.

I wrote this book for me and all the women and men out there that believe in the kind of love that blinds you from anyone else. The love that opens your eyes to that soulmate, and closes your eyes to any other person that tries to come between you.

God and I have struggled since the death of my dad, and again when my sister got sick, then sadly passing away too. I witnessed a miracle first hand when God answered our prayers, and she woke up after the physicians told us there was nothing left to do. That made me open my eyes and love God again.

I watched the once in a lifetime love that her husband had for her, and it reminded me that I needed to finish this story for them both.

My dad and my sister. Two of the best people I've ever known, loved with all their heart, and were loved by their perfect match. So, here's to the fairytale, unconditional, soulmate love.

I hope you can feel Atlanta and Dare's love as I did, while I was writing it. Close your eyes and know that we all deserve to be loved 100% of someone's heart. Never questioning the way a man or woman feels for us, because true love never gives us reasons to doubt it.

Thank you for reading, and may you always have someone who would follow you anywhere.

Christy Dilg

Stairs to you

BY: CHRISTY DILG

May you always have a love that will follow you anywhere.

♡ CDilg

Dedication

TO MY DAD AND SISTER: THANK YOU FOR LOVING ME
AS MUCH AS I LOVED YOU.

Best Friends

I am the only guy standing on the disco-lit dance floor next to a dozen screaming girls near the front of the small stage in a room that smells of booze and cheap women. Most men might enjoy a one nighter with any one of these ladies but I don't go for the screaming, over the top girls. I'm the guy that is interested in the one that is swaying back and forth feeling the music usually in the back of the room or alone at the table sipping on a long neck bottle. My best friend, Atlanta Lane Reed belts out her new single "Flying" while the entire room vibrates from the chants of her fans, word for word along with her.

We have been best friends since we were five and met at the local daycare. I will never forget when she strolled into the playroom, her chestnut brown hair sectioned in pigtails that dangle in front of her, and glassy blue eyes peaking up at me as I handed her my yellow transformer.

Sixteen years later, and she still has no indication I am insanely in love with her and have been ever since she stole my juice box years ago at lunchtime. She was a bully, but she always had my back unless there was something she wanted from me. What she didn't know was that I would have given her anything. I, Archer "Dare" Andrews, would give her everything even now.

Atlanta began singing at the age of eight during our school talent show. Her parents took notice, as well as the head of the chorus department. He added her to part of the school choir and as a result, I joined the band to be near her. Drums were the only instrument available that year, so I had no choice but to learn to play if I wanted to be spend extra time with her.

I followed through playing the drums until we graduated high school. No one ever knew how much I hated playing. All I needed was for her to look at me once without the friendship glasses on and fall head over heels for me. I have watched her go through boyfriend after boyfriend and I even tried to find love somewhere else but no matter how hard I looked, it was her face that I saw when I closed my eyes at night.

I never had the nerve to tell her my true feelings, because with my luck if I did she would stop answering my calls and avoid me at all turns. A life as Atlanta Reed's friend is better than any life without her.

Never seeing her face again would be the death of me. I couldn't jeopardize it. Therefore, I continue to portray the part of her best friend, so I can watch her laugh over the dumbest videos and replay the same little kid clip, where he hits his dad in the face and takes over his account.

Once her show is over, we go back to her apartment so I can help her finish a song she is struggling with.

Her tiny one bedroom apartment is on the third floor of her Uncle Damon's music store, which was passed down by Damon's grandfather. They still carry old records which take up the entire second floor.

From the back entrance leading to her apartment, we climb into a secret passage from her bedroom closet that leads to the second floor. Atlanta and I sneak down after-hours and jam out to the timeless classics on vinyl. She finds the inspiration to pour her heart out on paper here. The room smells of incense and it takes you back to the days where life was simple the minute you inhale the stale scent mixed with new fragrances. Atlanta and I have grown up loving this place that her great-grandfather built and Damon has managed to keep the feel of a sixties record store yet having the modern day music and technology for all the teenagers and millennium crowd.

The best nights of my life have been spent working on lyrics together in this place, so many they are countless.

Tonight will be another night to be remembered. Atlanta never entrusts anyone with her music until she is completely satisfied with every word-- except me, which makes me feel special. Her band called "Freak Switch" will help with the sheet music once she has completed the lyrics. She treats each song as a delicate baby, carefully cradling it until it can walk alone.

I stroll over to a small desk that is on the far end of the room and grab a notepad that is sitting on a stack of old newspaper clippings from when the store first opened. Atlanta switches the lamp light on and I take a seat on the black futon placing my chin in the palm of my hand as I flip through the pages of the notebook searching for a clear page. Atlanta's long brown hair hangs down as she leans over me reaching for the notepad in my hand.

"Hey, that's private." She declares as she swats my hand and grips the side of the paper before pulling it away from me.

"Since when do you have private things that I can't see?" My tone cracks from disappointment but my words are filled with surprise.

"Since now. I'm writing a new song for someone special and they can't see it." She pauses before playfully lunging at me and grabbing the notebook from my tight grip. "You, okay, and it's not ready". Her voice soft and childlike. She presses the worn pad into her stomach wrapping her arms around it so I can't pull it from her.

I have to admit I am flattered beyond words. My hand clinches at my shirt as I let the words sink in that she wrote a song for me. My heart skips a beat just before I try to snatch the notepad again from her tight gripped arms. When Atlanta writes a song it comes from somewhere deep inside her so you know if the words are about you then either you pissed her off or made her feel a sense of happiness. My hands are sweaty from the nerves in my body that are kinked up from the anticipation of what she has wrote and guys shouldn't get sensitive around anyone, especially a girl as my dad always would say. They will either think you are a pansy, or they will expect it more and I am not sure which is worse. Okay, so being a sissy has to be worse, but I don't want to sit around and watch chick flicks as we cry together, once the man finally does some heroic act of love. Yeah, that's just not going to happen. I still have balls somewhere.

I stare into her crystal blues eyes for a moment, before pulling my gaze away from her and play it off as no big deal.

But it is.

I don't want to give away my true feelings, or the fact I am secretly wishing the words will express her abiding love for me. I know it is a friendship song and nothing more. The last dagger to my heart, the goodbye to a future. She has never looked at me in a romantic way and her lips have never came close to grazing mine. I am just a lovesick fool, waiting for a fantasy, a dream that may never come true and let's get real; I'm not going to give up.

We spend the remainder of the evening in the large wood paneled room playing record after record off the old turntable that sits on the only table in the room until we finally play one that sparks the fire in our hearts, and moves the words in our minds making us dance. If you can't feel the music enough to get up and move to the beat, then you should keep listening to more songs until you do. Good music will speak to you, and when it does, you will dance.

Our song of the night is a slow love song from 1964. We jump up from futon and dance around the dim lit room, dodging the records dispersed all over the brown shag carpet. Her laughter fills the room, and creeps into my heart and we sway back and forth as I twirl her around and around like a ballerina. Her smile mesmerizes my mind and captivates me, then for a moment, my heart slams into my chest and I think I see that gaze I have been searching for all these years.

I freeze for a moment and search for it again. Is it so or have I fooled myself into thinking she might have taken the friendship glasses off? Nah, that dream has long since passed.

Since we pulled an all-nighter finalizing the song, I crashed on Atlanta's couch. Sitting up off the hard as steel yellow couch, I massage my neck to relieve the crick I developed on the side of it.

The clock on the wall indicates I have a little over an hour to get to Edward's Customs for work. It isn't glamorous, but being a mechanic pays the bills. It will only take about ten minutes to get there from Atlanta's place so I ease back into the worn in cushion. The best thing about living in Nashville is the music, but I think everything being nearby is a close second. Music Row is the heart of it all, and as a result, the record store fits in perfectly. Atlanta and her freaks play for a bar or club at least three times a week when she isn't touring which makes her apartment the perfect location for her.

Atlanta is still sleeping so I tip toe quietly into her obscure bedroom pausing for a moment, less than a stalker would, but just enough that I notice her chest moving slowly up and down with every breath as I slip into the bathroom to take a quick shower. I brush my teeth with the toothbrush I leave here in case I have to stay over. It happens so often I even have my own drawer. After I shower, I brush my dark hair, combing it to flip in the front and a mess in the back. Atlanta styled my hair this way a couple years ago. You would think I woke up like this, but it actually takes work to look this lazy. Once I am back in her room I open my drawer at the bottom of the large white dresser in the attempt to be quiet but I feel her eyes on me. "Good morning." I whisper without looking back at her then turn my body slightly to see her face.

"Are you off to work already," She queries before leaning up on her red satin pillows.

"Yeah, we are remodeling a 1967 mercury comet this week and I can't wait to get started on it," My tone sounds like a kid who just found the prize in the Cracker Jack box.

I don't have to act like the cool uninterested guy. With her, I can be myself. I appreciate the comfort I feel when we are together, but mostly I love being the one that can always make her smile, even on her worst day. The power of knowing I can brighten her mood with one tiny blow of air on the crease of her elbow makes me smile. I found that sensitive spot when we were twelve years old and she tackled me to the ground trying to get the last candy bar. I tried tickling her or even pushing her off, but I was never forceful enough because let's face it, I wanted the attention. After several attempts of trying to get her to release the nutty candy, I blew in her face, which made her angry and me laugh. A short while later I blew on the crease inside her elbow, then her whole demeanor changed and she couldn't stop laughing.

That's when I knew I had a secret weapon for life. It saved my candy then, and now I know I can use it whenever I want to see her smile.

I tell her goodbye after we make plans to hang out tomorrow night once her set is over and play a car racing game on her game box. Fast cars obsess us both and on the weekend, you can find us at the drag racing track just outside the city. Currently, I drive a blue 1995 Chevrolet truck that my parents got me when I turned sixteen years old so we race Atlanta's white 1967 Chevrolet Camero ZL1, 427 horsepower, with a V-8 engine. Her car is fast, but we are just amateurs and haven't ever made it far in the races, usually placing last. We mainly go so we can get a close up of all the cars.

Every weekend someone new shows up claiming to be the fastest, and some even finish nearly in the top five. Once I pull into the garage, I notice a matte black 1970 dodge challenger parked in the front of the building. My dream car.

I remember as a young boy flipping through my dad's muscle car magazines and always stopping on the challenger. I swear I would even drool a little. I pull into the parking spot around back and make my way to check out the beauty making my heart skip more than one beat. As I round the corner and I get a clear glimpse of her, my knees buckle a little.

Classic Beauty

A gorgeous blonde girl walks out of the office door with Edward, my boss. I can't take my eyes off the car, but I become aware of them walking toward me. "Like what you see?" The blonde questions.

"Who wouldn't?" I call out. The car has red lettering and a small red pinstripe trimming the body. Chrome surrounds it in all the perfect places. The gas cap, letters, steering wheel, gearshift and the star chrome rims also have red inserts that match the red lining the car.

"Wanna see under the hood?" She questions while opening the driver side door and pulling the release.

"You bet." I half nod before walking to the front of the car and propping up the hood, revealing the reflective engine that sits in the center. Once it is secure, I stand back a little to get the full view of the beast running the beauty. It has an aluminum hemi backed by a 5-speed manual transmission and the custom job on her is off the chain. Red and chrome colors span the car with no grit of dirt in sight. "This is a man's dream." I whisper to myself, but she hears me and responds.

"But it's a woman's car." She props her hand on her hip before leaning on the bumper of the car, her movement flirty yet subtle. "I want to sell it. Wanna make an offer?"

I can't help but laugh. Cars like this sell in the hundred thousand range and though it is worth every cent, I'm just a grease monkey and the last thing I have is that kind of dough, "I can't afford this car, but thanks for offering." I close the hood and back away, "I have to get to work. Thank you again ma'am for letting me check her out. She is impressive."

"As are you, Dare. A man with a strong jaw line and the ability to make a work of art from metal is very impressive." She gushes and I hear a sense of flirtatious vibes from her tone.

I grin then turn and let myself in the front door of the office, but need to take just one last look at my dream car. I let the glass door firmly close shut, then turn and lean my head on the glass and take it in before sauntering off to the break room. The break room looks more like a dump than a place you are supposed to sit down and eat, but what should I expect out of a bunch of grease monkeys like myself. I need some coffee, black and quick. The sludge pours down my throat, heating my vocal pipes on the way down. As I lean against the white counter, the door opens and in strides the blonde-haired woman from outside.

"My name is Camry by the way. You know like the car. Apparently, I was conceived in the back seat of my grandma's car," She confesses, rolling her eyes before walking in and taking a seat at the rectangle table stacked with condiments for the lunch crowd. She apparently don't take no for an answer. I sigh.

She crosses her long tan legs and leans her elbows on the table. "I have a proposition for you," She pauses for me to take interest in her, but I only have eyes for one girl and she isn't blonde or sitting in this room. "Don't you want to hear what it is?" she tries again. This time I shrug my shoulders, tilting my head to the side.

"What's on your mind?" I question, and move to sit across from her. Her blue eyes meet mine and I catch her take in a deep breath. Is she nervous? The deep breath and way her hands are fidgeting lead me to believe that I make her nervous but she's still wanting to flirt with me some more. I can't for the life of me understand why Edward let her back here.

"My dad built this car for five years and it was complete right before he was diagnosed with ALS. He is unable to drive it now and has been confined to a wheel chair for the past year. I need someone to drive it at the race track so he can see it in action," Her voice cracks a little but she pushes through, "Edward, told me you were the man for the job. If you do this the car is yours-- one pink slip for one awesome race." Her eyes glisten with moistness from the tears building up.

"I don't know what to say. I'm sorry about your dad, but I can't take his car for one race. That wouldn't be fair. I'll drive the car, because it would be an honor to help your dad get to see his hard work get into the groove and gain traction." My voice is filled with empathy.

"I would like you to race the car this weekend. I'm scared if I wait much longer my dad will never see it," her eyelids close releasing a single tear.

"I'll need to practice tonight and tomorrow to be ready for Saturday. I'm not the best driver, but my friend and I race her car for fun. I want to make sure you understand I'm not a winner. No racing star here. I am just a guy that loves fast cars. I can't guarantee I would even place. Heck, out of all the times I have been on that track I still haven't placed," Atlanta's car is fast, but I always chicken out at the last minute and ease up on the pedal. I am so afraid I will pull too hard or not quick enough and with Atlanta by my side; I could never take that chance.

Growing up I got the nickname, Dare, in the fourth grade, when dared by a bully to jump off the monkey bars at recess, and despite my fear, I climbed up on the top of the metal bars and stood looking down below. All the kids surrounded it to watch me cry and climb down. The bully, Steven, was chanting chicken and I knew I had to do it. Not just for me, but also for all the kids he bullied every day at recess and during the bus rides to school. I took in a deep breath and jumped off the bar onto the dirt. The only thing I remember was pain. Unbearable pain. I heard my bones snap in two and I started screaming from the pain. You could barely hear my screaming over Steven's laughter, but a teacher had seen me fall, and ran over to check on me. From that day forward, I did every dare someone challenged to prove I was tough. I mean when you cry like a girl, you don't look manly to the ladies. However, no matter how many dares I did, everyone still knew me as the sissy who jumped off those monkey bars and cried like a girl.

Years later when I was in high school I was challenged my final dare by that same bully that grew up to be one of my best friends. This time the dare wasn't as physically dangerous but instead it was emotionally hazardous. He knew my feelings for Atlanta and dared me to tell her. Let's just say I am still on that dare and maybe one day I will accomplish it and move on to the next one. I am terrified of breaking something else and I fear that it will put me through more pain than the broken leg ever did if she doesn't feel the same. A broken heart has to ache worse than a bone any day.

"If you drive me home, you can keep the car to practice and I will see you Saturday at the track, before the race I want to reassure you that this is about my dad watching the one thing he worked so hard on finally hit the track and not about you being the best.

Edward said you were the best man for the job because he trust you and that is enough for me" Camry offers, uncrossing her legs and standing up from the table.

"I'll have to talk to Ed and see if it's okay with him. I am on the clock, ya know," I rise, usher her out of the break room, and follow behind her to the front office. Ed is on the phone so we wait. I glance over at her and wonder how she could even contemplate giving up the car. It is her father's baby. Something he built for years because of his passion of cars. She must really care for him to make this happen. She is no older than I am and yet she seems to be so together. It's not just her daddy's money either. I can see she is determined and gets things done. I love when a woman knows what she wants in life. Atlanta is the same way.

Growing up all she wanted was to be a singer and travel from place to place, captivating audiences with her words. She started performing in clubs in high school with her band, The Freaks. She made a name for herself around town and last year she signed on with Smash Records, her first album went gold, and after the tour finished she insisted that she play in the small bars.

She said she never wants to lose the person she was before the fame and she still lives in the same apartment above her uncle's music store even though she can afford to buy a larger place of her own. I think a lot of the reason is that she doesn't like change. She has never bought a CD still to this day because she hates new things. Other than her phone and game console, I don't think she has any other new technology at her house. Right down to the twist and turn can opener. She lives simple except for her car. It is a classic, and it was not a cheapie. The minute she got her first paycheck from her tour, she put down almost ninety thousand dollars for her ride.

It is fast, but the challenger sitting outside will out run her any day. I have a strange feeling she will be up for a race and who better to practice with.

Ed finally hangs up the phone. "Hey Ed, Camry would like me to drive her home if that is okay and she is going to let me keep her car for a few days." His jaw drops and I am sure I heard his bone pop as it hit the counter.

"Has she lost her mind? She doesn't know you from Adam." he glances over at her. "Camry, what makes you think he will give you the car back in one piece?" he pauses for her answer, leaning on the wood stool behind him.

"Well..." her eyes flicker to me and back to Ed. "After this weekend, it will be his car so I won't need it back and Ed, you did say he was the man for the job," she continues before walking out the door. Ed glares at me as if I just slapped a baby. I shrug my shoulders. "This is what she wants. I already told her no, but she won't listen. I'll talk to you about it when I get back," he nods and I leave to drive her home. I open the driver's side door and admire the black leather seats trimmed in red. The top of the black seat has embroidered in red the words "Live it".

There are so many ways you could interpret the meaning behind them. If I had to put my two cents in to the pot, I would say it means live your dream and personally; I need to work on that. I have let my dream of being with Atlanta fall into the external friend zone. I've lived in regret every day from not at least attempting to be with her. As for my other dream of cars, I live it every day. You would never catch me pushing paper in some nine to five job. Cars are my life. Atlanta is my life. I might not be able to afford to buy one of them but being a mechanic on classic beauties lets me drive a new one every week and sometimes more than that.

I get to pimp each one to the fullest and around here, our customers are the kind with no price limit so it's not as if we have to take the cheap way out. We have regulars that come to us and we take an old rusted model they have bought at an auction and turn into a one of a kind custom hundred thousand dollar beauty. I get to watch the reactions they have when they first lay eyes on the finished project and hear them squeal from excitement when they turn the key for the first time. That is living. Seeing others' dreams come true and enjoying each classic that pulls in and out of this garage. Not to mention Ed lets me take off a moment's notice so I can travel with Atlanta to her shows.

"So, what do you do for fun other than race cars?" Camry twist her head towards me, her eyes watching my face.

"My best friend is a singer so I watch her perform a few times a week and play a lot of video games." I answer not giving her too many details."

"Any girlfriends?"

"A few here and there but nothing serious." I tell her.

"Maybe that will change soon?" Her tone becomes sensual.

"Doubtful. My heart is already taken by someone that doesn't know it yet."

Camry nods slightly but don't reply to my statement. I notice out of the corner of my eye that she's thinking on it by the way she is biting her lip just like Atlanta does.

"I am the first house on the left." Camry directs me. She gathers her purse and sits it on her lap. A wrought iron gate with stone columns borders the house. I pull the car up the driveway and stop at the closed gate. "1226 is the code. Don't tell all your friends." She jokes.

"No way girl. I would never jeopardize this deal for a gate code. Do I look like I am brainless?" I assure her jokingly.

Camry's house is a brick colonial style mansion and when I say mansion I am talking about the kind that is on "MTV's Cribs" and even though the place could fit an elementary school inside it, I try to keep my cool. I live in a small mobile home on the outskirts of Nashville, but I have some class and keeping your dignity intact when you roll up on something grand like this is step one. I pull the car up the circle driveway and park it near the front door.

I turn the car off, before I jump out and walk around to the passenger side to open her door. "Don't mind the oversized house and staff. My parents did well for themselves then two years ago, my mom ran off to be with a young ballet instructor from my dance school. This is my dad's house. He left everything the same as the day she left him. I haven't spoken to her since she called to tell me she wasn't coming back to us and a year later he was diagnosed with ALS." Camry's voice cracks more as the words spill from her pale pink lips. "It's okay, really. In the long run my dad and I are better off without someone that could disappear from our lives so easily."

My heart aches for her. "I'm sorry to hear about that, but glad to see you haven't let money or your mother leaving define who you are," I hold my hand out and help her out of the car.

"What's your story? Care to let me in?" she takes my hand and steps out of the car.

"Quick run through, I work on cars I can't afford and I'm in love with my best friend that only sees me as her friend."

She lets out a small puff of air, "Oh. Her loss," her big eyes peer up at me and then they fall toward the pathway. I close the car door and walk her to the porch. I was raised to be a gentleman and walking a lady to her door regardless of your relationship was always my mom's top rule.

"I will see you at the track. Can't wait to meet your dad," I turn and march back to the car. With every step, I admire the lines and history of the car.

"Hey," she yells to me. Reaching the car, I turn back and lean on the top it, waiting for her to continue.

"I'm serious about giving you the car. I don't want it," she smiles and turns walking into her house, closing the door behind her. Again, I wonder how she could so easily give up such a beautiful car. It isn't my place to ask her why. I stare at her front door clueless before opening the car door. The slick black leather seats feel warmed from the sun when I climb back in. It's as if Mr. Grant had them custom made just for me. The seats molding to my body when I relax into the sun warmed leather is how I would imagine a car that I custom made for myself. The man has style.

I turn the key and the sound of the engine enraptures me. I have to ride by Atlanta's before heading back to work even though we made plans for tomorrow night. I dig the cell phone out of my front pocket and click on her name.

She is stubborn, but she caves for me every time. Sometimes I think her nickname should have been Dare, but with a name like Atlanta, it's as if she already has a nickname. I roll the windows down and turn the radio up loud as I take the back roads to her apartment.

The car drives so smooth and the motor roars with the slightest touch of the pedal.

It doesn't take any time before I pull into the front of the Damon's music store. Parking the car, I walk to the back taking a glance at the large mosaic peace sign that takes up the entire side of the building. It has been there since the store opened including a sign that reads, 'Hippies take the back entrance'. People write their dreams on the colored tile pieces that create the design. Some days Atlanta and I stand here and read nearly every one. It puts your life in perspective. Knowing others have dreams too and none are too big or too small. I love the history that surrounds the town and this store. There are days I walk around admiring the city. Atlanta is sitting on the stairs when I round the corner. My blood begins to pump harder when I see her and my heart does back flips for a brief moment. *Damn she's beautiful.* She doesn't need the over the top makeup or clothes to enhance her beauty because she's stunning enough without it. The big man above sure made the perfect canvas when he created her.

"What's going on? It's not like you to come by when you should be at work," she jumps up and walks over to me.

"Follow me, Atlanta and I will show you," I grasp her small, soft hand and lead her to the front of the store.

Once we reach the car, I wave my hand like I am displaying it.

"Is this what you are working on now? You freaked me out," She punches my arm, "Dang, its sweet," she says with excitement, walking around looking at every inch of the car. After standing still long enough to get her attention, I go into detail about the proposal Camry had offered me earlier. Atlanta's crystal eyes widen and her mouth nearly hits the ground as I am explaining it, but she lets me finish before she lets out a crazy scream. She is so adorable when she tries to hold back her emotions until I finish.

She jumps up and down and grabs my hands just before throwing hers around my neck. I can't help but take in every second of this moment with her arms around me. I can feel the heat overtake my body. "Finally, you get your dream," she squeals, backing away and opening the car door. Little does she know she is my real dream!

"I am a little jealous. I don't have custom seats in mine. They feel like they mold to your body," She envy's "they feel like a soft pillow memory foam cushion. I have to get some of these. Maybe, if I get lucky on my next album," she continues.

"Yeah, I thought they were made for me when I sat in them and that is coming from the one that custom makes the memory foam seats alongside my buddy John; I should have known the difference. Guess I was blinded by love," I poke fun at myself. She laughs. Man, I love the sound of her laughter; the kind that pulls me in no matter what mood I am in and tugs hard at my heart. I wish for one second she would see me as someone that could be her husband; the man that she would want to spend the rest of her life with and create a family together.

I thought she had the second I looked into her eyes last night, but Atlanta isn't someone that holds back. If it were there she would have told me or at least I think she would have told me.

"Do you want to practice with me tonight at the track? I have two days to get to know this car and run it hard," I ask as she closes the car door behind her.

"So…no game night?" She teases.

I chuckle, "No, no game night."

"Well duh! I will meet you at the track at…six," She grins, "do you think this has an edge over my car?" She tilts her head toward the Challenger.

"It will be close," I don't want to make her think less of her car. "It is Bad Ass." She smirks.

"Well, it's on," we say goodbye after I walk her to her door. I have to get back to work or Ed is going to think I did trash the car. Of course he knows I can be trusted with any car, but I have been gone an hour so surely he is starting to worry.

Ed has been my boss since I was the age of fifteen and begged him to hire me. I was at the legal age to start working and the last place I wanted to be was a fast food joint or bagging groceries with the dorky kids from school. He took me under his wing, and became like a second dad to me and taught me everything he knew. One day I hope to buy the business from him when he finally decides to retire. Until then I am happy working alongside him.

When I return to work, Ed joins me in the garage next to the Mercury Comet I'm working on and quizzes me down like a teenage girl's best friend about a date.

"Dare, what are you going to do?" Ed gazed at me with concern.

"Dude, stuff like this doesn't come around except once in a lifetime if you are lucky, and this week, I just happen to be at the end of the brightest rainbow with a pot of gold sitting there waiting for me to grab it. I'm not telling her no again." I lean into the hood and unscrew the water pump so I can replace it with a new one. Ed finally eases up on me and shakes his head.

"I get it son, I just don't understand who could give up a car like that at no price," he places two hands firmly on the side of the car I am working on and looks over the motor, "this is coming along quickly. The owner will be pleased to get it back so fast. I can't believe we are lining the entire car inside and out in pink. It gives me the chills just thinking about it. A pink comet. Man it just ain't right," Ed turns and strolls back to his office. I gaze over at Marty, one of the mechanics helping with this project. He is a short guy with red hair, but he can have you laughing your butt off at his jokes or all around goofiness.

He rolls his eyes and murmurs, "pink."

I assure him, it could be worse. It could be polka dotted with little kitties," we both laugh and shake our heads at the thought.

3
Flag Girl

I was leaning against the car for about ten minutes when she pulled into the paved parking lot. I wave for her to drive down to the pit, so we can see what this car can do. When she steps out, I notice she is wearing her 'Flag girl' shoes. Wowzer! She wears these sexy as hell boots that come up to her thighs, jet-black leather with a four or five inch heel. The material almost covers her entire leg, but gives you a small peek of skin until you reach her short black skirt. She is hot and I mean smoking hot, but she is so much more than just her body. This girl has a soul like no one I have ever witnessed and her outside beauty is enriched by it. She has a red scarf tied around her neck that barely touches the top of her black tank top. I can't help but think about how my lips would feel on her neck as I glance at the fabric softly touching her bare skin. She pulls off a new generation of 'Sandy' from the old time classic movie very well and I know the sequel would out sell the original. I of course, am biased, but I'm sure the world would see it my way once they get a glimpse of her.

"Are you ready to see how this car handles?" I call out to her as she strolls toward me. Man, she looks stunning. I could take a photo of this moment and carry it with me until the end of time, but a photo of this moment could never capture my pulse beating at 9000 rpms. I swear she can see it pumping out of my chest.

My hands are sweaty and my heart beats faster with every breath I take.

"Heck yeah. I've been ready since I heard the proposal," she leans over and kisses me on the cheek as she does before every race, "good luck," she backs away and walks over to the red light pole, which some people call a Christmas tree.

I climb into the car and put on my seatbelt, slide the key into the ignition, and crank the car. The engine purrs effortlessly. Muscle cars have a sound you feel inside your chest, and it almost fuels it, giving you a desire to push the pedal hard.

The vibrations of the motor are working to make every inch of the box work to the best of its ability. The car is prone. I turn my gaze to Atlanta just as I shift the lever into gear and produce a thumb's up so she knows I'm ready.

She switches the tree from yellow to green and I push the pedal vigorously leaving a thick cloud of smoke behind me. I am almost to the second turn and my heart is pumping rapidly as I hit one hundred and ten miles an hour. It is exhilarating when the car reaches higher speeds, but I hold steady. It's a moment of solitude out here on the track alone. I can lose myself while I am out here on this black track with no one to pass or nudge out of my way. It's a total adrenaline rush. After the second lap the light flicks to red, so I slow down and pull into the pit area. Atlanta tugs on the scarf around her neck and it slides off smoothly, shaking it in the air beside her.

Atlanta begins asking questions before I get out of the car, "wow that car is fast. You drove it as if you have driven it before. What did you think?"

I can't help but laugh at her excitement. It is just endearing. When you grow up with someone you begin to know things no one else does and learn what each emotion means to them. When she is happy, the inner child comes to life inside her and she reacts with merriment. I love that she can be childish at the exciting times in our lives. Some women are either over the top dumb or too serious. Atlanta has just enough of each that it creates the perfect woman.

My perfect woman.

The way she smells, the way she twists her lips when she is thinking, her voice, and soul. When am I going to stop being a coward and tell her how I feel? I want more from her than friendship--I want forever.

"It was awesome. The power the car has is incredible. Wanna give it a try?" I ask her, knowing what her answer will be.

"That's a dumb question," she darts for the car, dropping her scarf on the way. I pick it up before I make my way to the Christmas tree and set the light to yellow. She looks good sitting in that car and I can't help but feel somewhat anxious as she clicks the seat belt into place around her sexy ass body.

When she is ready, she does her signature deuces hand sign and I flick the light to green. She rounds the first turn seamlessly and picks up momentum around the second curve.

When we race on Saturday we will be driving on the straight track, but I wanted to get a feel of how the car handles curves and slants in the road so we are testing her out here first.

Atlanta is driving about one hundred and thirty when I flick on the red light. I know she would push it harder but let's face it, I am very cautious when it comes to her safety. This car does have a roll bar on top since it was made for racing, which is an added bonus nevertheless I'm not taking any chances. She pulls up and turns the car off. She has a grin on her face from ear to ear and I am sure she is bouncing in the seat, "Ahh. This car is BA. You're going to win. I can feel it," she gushes after stepping out of the car. I turn the tree off and make my way over to her. She flings her arms around my neck and jumps up and down with excitement. Her hair tickles my nose a bit so I tilt my head back and then I nuzzle my face into her hair, taking in a deep breath. Her hair smells like the clean floral scent of the shampoo I use when I shower at her house. I end up smelling like a girl, but I never care, because her scent surrounds me when it is on my skin and it is intoxicating.

"I can't wait to see how it does on the strip. I'm going to take it tomorrow night and try it out. I'll probably miss have to miss your performance," once the words come out of my mouth, her face changes from joyful to utterly shocked. I have never missed a show no matter how big or how small, "I'll be at the next one. I promise. I just need to make sure that I'm primed for Saturday. I don't want Camry's dad to be let down, because I am a bad driver. You know I chicken out at the end," I confess.

"I know. It's not that, I just wish I were here with you. I could always cancel," she rolls her eyes to the side and smooches her lips together, "I can't do that, but I am going to be so sad so I guess I'll play a lot of sappy songs," she giggles and releases my neck.

"I'll come by after I finish here," I assure her. I grab her hand in mine that is cool from the night air and walk her toward her car, "be careful driving home. I need you with me Saturday." She gets in her car and I watch her drive out safely, before I drive home.

The next day I awoke to the annoying alarm ringing in my ear. On most mornings I wouldn't mind getting up and starting my daily routine but the dream I was having was better than any car I was working on at the garage.

Atlanta and I were camping and the last thing I remember before the buzzing was the glow from the fire on her face. She's hot in every light but in that dream she was mesmerizing. I can almost smell the hickory wood burning as I recall every second of the dream before my mind forgets it. She leaned in and kissed me then just like every other moment something interrupted. This time it was reality.

Work flew by and afterward I drove the car to the track. I had called earlier to ensure I would be the only one there practicing, but when I pulled in a few younger guys are there with their cars. I am aggravated, but I don't want to initiate anything. I park and stride over to the men to see what they are doing. I am good friends with the owner so I can't imagine he knows they are here or he would have called me. I start by introducing myself to the man closest to the first car I see, "hey, I'm Dare.

Are you all practicing for the race tomorrow night?" I ask, offering my hand to shake. He completely ignores me and I let my hand fall to my side. Taken back I try again, "have you raced here before. I've never seen you around," this time I get his attention as well as the others in the group.

"Yeah, we are here for the race tomorrow. What's it to you?" an older blonde bows his chest up like he was going to show me a little something if I got rude. I am sure they all have a chip on their shoulder. This is not where I should be alone but I don't back down from no one.

Where is my posse when I need them? "I just wanted to introduce myself. I reserved the track tonight from the owner. Does he know you are here?" I ask firmly, trying to steer them off.

"No, we thought it was available to anyone," the blonde one responds. Still not one of them has introduced them self to me. I don't know what the point is to be such buttheads.

"Are you from around here?" I question in hopes they will lighten up.

"No, we are from Georgia. My name is Tucker," the tallest one with dark hair comes from behind the blonde-haired guy, "this is Ryan and Buck," he points to the others.

"Nice to meet you all. Good luck tomorrow! I guess I will leave y'all to practice," I wave and turn to walk back to my car.

I get a vibe that the other two are not as friendly as Tucker and the last thing I need is to show up with a black eye or swollen hand when I see Atlanta. She will never let me out of her sight again and in some ways that is good, but a man still needs his space. The two guys never say a word, but Tucker yells bye before I get into my car.

Atlanta is already on stage when I get there. Tonight she is performing at a new bar called, Mouth, we love it here. She performed in the sister bar down in Palm Coast, Florida last year and the owner decided to franchise. What better place is there to have a karaoke bar than Music Row? It is only a few stores down from Atlanta's apartment, which makes it perfect for us. It is also a grill so we have been coming here a couple nights a week to eat since it opened a few weeks ago. I can't help but laugh. The microphone has big huge "Steven Tyler" lips on it, which makes anyone look hilarious but him. I have to get a photo of her so I pull my cell phone out of my pocket and walk close to the stage. I hold the phone extremely still as I snap a photo of her. She gives me a stare that means I am definitely going to pay for it later. I laugh as I walk to the bar to order a beer. I grab my beer and sit at a table close to the stage.

Atlanta's tattoos on her arm pop tonight in her red top. I have never been brave enough to get a tattoo and she teases me all the time about it. She has an entire sleeve done, and more tattoos on several other areas of her body. When I see her in the tiny tank tops she wears and it reveals her ink I have to admit I find myself a little turned on. I almost did one and ended up chickening out after they placed the tracing paper on my arm. Atlanta laughed at me for days; no, it was weeks before she finally let it go.

She sings for another hour and I think nine girls came up to the table and asked me to dance. After several maybe's and a few hell no's I glance up at Atlanta on stage doing the thing she does best and I lose myself in her words. I haven't heard this new song before. Oh, my…is this the song for me?

He is my rock

My go to, my everything

I sit back and wait

Wait for him to see me.

Every day we are together

He overlooks my heart

Never touching my lips

We're just friends going through the motions

See me, love me

Why can't you hold me?

I don't want to be apart

I want to be in your heart

I'm going through the motions

Why can't you see me like I see you?

Grab me fast or I will disappear

I'm begging here, See me.

No, this is not the song for me. I do wonder if it has any meaning behind it. Is there a new guy that I don't know about or an old one she still cares for? I continue racking my brain, but I never take my eyes off her. She is breathtaking on and off stage, but the stage gives her balance and releases something in her that only comes out under the lights. It's captivating. I am the only man that I can picture being her rock. I don't understand, is she trying to tell me something or am I grasping at straws? This set is the longest one she has ever performed other than when she was on tour.

I have to get another beer so I flag down the waitress. A cute brown-haired woman walks over carrying extra beers and sits one down on the table. I hand her a five and tell her to keep the change. I take a sip and then chug the rest. I am not a big drinker but right now, I am too confused to be sober. I hold up my hand to the server and she brings over another one. Atlanta is concentrating on me hard and her facial expression is sad. As I take a swig of beer, I am reminded of the words she sang, 'Grab me fast, or I will disappear'. Tonight is the night. Whether it is for me or some lucky guy, I am telling her tonight that I love her-- that my world isn't complete until she loves me back.

She strides off the stage and packs her guitar when her set is over. She stops and signs some autographs for fans that have barricaded her in a corner. Her eyes glance over to me for a brief moment and back to her fans.

I stand up, march over to where she is standing, and push myself through the crowd. I don't know what has gotten into me, but I grab her by her petite shoulders firmly and she gawks at me shocked and concerned as to what is wrong, "Atlanta Lane Reed, I love you. I have loved you since you stole my juice box. I am tired of waiting for you to love me.

I don't know if that song was meant for me, but it should be," I pull her lips to mine. Smashing our mouths together and wrapping my arms around her back. I wait for her to hit me, kick me, push me away, but instead she kisses me back. Her lips part and our tongues interweave together and hers enclose over mine repeatedly causing the heat to rise and crowd to vanish. Her hands entangle my hair, tugging slightly with every breath of air she takes in. I can taste the cherry bomb flavored lip-gloss on her lips as I suck on each one softly. We gradually pull away, our eyes peering into each other's.

In the slightest whisper she utters, "I love you."

I beam a shit-eating grin before I plant another kiss on her lips. I grab the guitar out of her hand, leading her out of the bar, "we should get out of here and go somewhere quiet," I say and my heart begins to race. We walk a few shops down, to Damon's store, ignoring the paparazzi as we and round the corner to the back entrance to her apartment. Neither of us speak as we make our way inside her place.

Too many emotions and thoughts are swarming inside our brains. What is going to happen to our friendship after the secrets have escaped our hearts?

I wonder how long she has felt this way. She knows now, that I have loved her since we were toddlers fighting over small plastic toys and she never knew or did she? I am dying to hear what she is feeling although at the same time, I am scared that on the brief walk to her place, she has changed her mind and the moment is lost. I twist my neck around and glance at her strikingly beautiful pale face with flushed cheeks from the hasty walk here and every inch of me heats. I love this woman.

From the depths of my soul, I love her. Please God, don't let her take it back. Fear sets in and questions flood me as she unlocks the blue-green door. What step do you take next with someone you have loved your whole life but never told? Do you date or have you essentially dated your whole life? I have several questions and so many countless fears.

4

Stubborn

Once we are inside Atlanta lays her keys in the glass fish bowl on the small white antique table sitting by the front door. The smell of the "Dance with Clouds" incense she burns before every show fills my lungs as I take in a deep breath to calm my nerves. A blend of mandarin oranges mixed with the essential oil Ylang Ylang immediately over takes my body and I shut the door behind me. I don't wait for her to speak, but instead I rush over to her, glide both my hands on either side of her face, peer in her eyes, and kiss her. The passion is too strong. I watched her date other men before, love them, and leave them and now it is my turn to have everything.

Her.

She is everything; the heartbeat that keeps me going, the spell that has been cast over me. I won't-- I can't wait any longer to taste her lips. Her hands grasp at the worn-out blue flannel shirt that clings to my back just as her mouth connects mine in the kiss. She tastes better than I have dreamt about all these years and her soft lips are plump, ravishing mine with so much desire. I don't know what we waited for, wasting time playing the doting best friends when we could have been together. Heck, we might have been married by now if we both weren't so stubborn.

I pull away gradually from our kiss but, I leave my hands on her soft face. "I've been waiting my whole life to do that and now that it's transpired twice, I don't want to stop, but I need to know what is in your head. When did this happen for you?" I slide my hands from her face, down her bare arms and lightly stroked her hands in mine. My breath quickens once I feel the warmth of her skin.

Her blue eyes glisten with held back tears and this saddens me. "I knew a few months ago after I called you for the twentieth time at three o'clock in the morning after Wesley dumped me. You came right over and comforted me, no questions asked and you never once complained about the late hour. We were lying on the couch and you were rubbing my feet in your lap as we watched a car show on the discovery channel.

I was watching your fingers sliding over the soles of my bare feet when the thought registered in my mind about what our life would be like if we never met. Thinking about my life without you felt like gutting my heart out without anesthesia." I brushed my hand over her cheek. "I've always loved you but in that moment, I let myself fall in love with you. Every minute since, I have been falling in deeper and deeper terrified you wouldn't feel the same way. I started writing the words on paper and once I felt they were complete I knew tonight was the night to perform it. I didn't know you would know it was about you, but I hoped you would," her voice cracked as she opened her heart to me. "I wished every night for you to feel the way I did. We have been friends for so long I feared we would change, but at the same time I also believe we were meant to be."

She pauses long enough for me to get a word in, "Why were we so stupid? Three months went by since you finally opened your eyes to what has been in front of your sweet face all these years."

I shift my legs and brush my thumb across her cheek again. "We have been friends long enough that I know we wouldn't let it hurt what we have if it was to fail, but sugar, I don't see us failing." Her lips press against mine and we both let out a small chuckle at the strangeness of it. "It's a little weird kissing huh?" I whisper as I back my lips away from hers. "But it feels right," Atlanta murmurs just before pressing her soft lips against mine.

After all these years of wanting to be with her like this, the feelings take over. I can't stop kissing her and from the looks of it, she feels the same way. It's weird, but at the same time it is as if we have been doing it our whole lives. Not wanting to move from this spot, but knowing we need to talk about things before we escalate to the next level, I back away slowly, take her hand, and pull her to the plush couch and we sit. She leans her back into my chest and spreads her legs along the rest of the couch. Even though we have sat like this more times than I can count, this time feels different. Almost like, I woke up in Heaven and she was there waiting for me. Standing outside the pearly gates and reaching out for my hand so she could escort me inside to a place our imaginations could never think up. It is magnificent beyond our wildest dreams. That is what this moment feels like on this old yellow couch with her by my side.

"So where do we go from here? A date or do we move past all the getting to know each other and straight to the girlfriend/boyfriend aspect?" I ask her while I stroke her hair off her forehead. She grasps my arm around her waist and squeezes it gently.

"I think we should go on one date just to say we did and one won't hurt. I mean haven't we already done everything a couple could do on a date?" Atlanta playfully bats her blue eyes.

Her eyes flick up toward me as she tilts her head back just enough to see my facial expression. "You are right. So where would you like this date to take place? From your tone I think you have something in mind." I inquire before I lean in and kiss the top of her head. She chuckles and shifts her body to face me. "So…you see, Danielle asked if we would go to the opening of her art studio Sunday evening and well…I really want to go," she bats her impeccable blue eyes and her naturally pink lips twist up in a devilish smile because she knows she got her way.

"Of course we will go. We would have either way but we can call it a date," I utter.

Danielle is our dear friend that we have known since high school. She went on to art school in New York, but moved back here when her mom became ill. Six months after returning home her mom died from colon cancer.

It has been a year since she passed away and after months of being broken Dani is ready to open her own studio filled with paintings she has been working on since she moved back home. Atlanta has seen a few finished paintings and told me they were deep, beautiful, but filled with great sadness. "We have to support her. We are all she has." I brush my thumb across her chin and she leans in to kiss me.

"True. I was going with or without you anyway. She is like a sister to me," her words trail off.

"Spill it," I demand in a firm tone, but smile with my eyes so she knows I mean it in the nicest way.

"I know it's dumb but I used to think of you like a brother and here we are making out on the couch your parents gave me when I first moved in here. What are our friends going to think?" Her words soften and I slide my hand over her ear tucking a loose strand of hair behind it.

"We live in the south so half the people in this area are kissing cousins anyway. It's going to be a relief that we aren't related by blood," I tease her trying to lighten the mood. I know our closest friends are going to be shocked but in all seriousness, we have been headed down this path our whole lives and whether we knew it or not our hearts were meant to love each other for eternity.

She nudges me slightly in the arm, her eyes beaming as her lips widen into a smile. "I suppose you are right. Dani already knows I have been behind the scenes pining for you these past few months anyway. She will be thrilled."

"I can't believe you told someone." I put my fist on my chest. "I feel special, like you like me a little." I smirk.

"Keep it up and I'll send you packing, drawer and all." She throws her hands on her hips and sits up on the couch, twisting toward me. Her face is squished in the most adorable pout. No one would resist it.

"You love me," I grin a large dorky teeth beaming grin. Leaning back in my arms and pulling her black fuzzy blanket up to her chest, she snuggles into me. "Ditto." I wrap my arms around her and sink into the couch. We found our place for the evening. As I drift off to sleep, I think about all the memories we have and all the ones we will continue to experience.

I'm ready. I'm ready for what is to come of our relationship and more than that, I am ready for there to be no more secrets. The time has come that I finally get my dream and it's going to be amazing. The butterflies are swimming in my stomach as my mind wonders. I stretch my arm out barely touching my other arm and I pinch myself just to be sure I'm not dreaming. It stings a little so I take in a deep breath and as I close my eyes for the evening, I smile to myself. This is real. With all the emotions that have been pent up and the ones that were released tonight there is one that I am controlling. The horn ball man emotion. All men have it but few can actually tame it. I've gotten good at this over the years. Now, things will probably change but tonight I'm chaining it up.

A small piercing light beams through the blinds of the window adjacent to the couch. When it hits my face my eyelids flinch. I squint as I pry them open. Atlanta is still snuggled up to my chest and her cute mouth is wide open as she breathes softly in and out. The stream of light touches her hair and enhances the reddish tint color. It fits her so well. Fiery and hot. She changes her hair quite often, but this is the best look yet. Of course, I say that every time. Heck, I even liked it when she had it multiple colors of blue, pink and purples. She stirs and her lips close before her tongue slips out and passes gently over the top and bottom lip, wetting them. She looks up at me, "Morning."

I grin and nuzzle my nose in her soft hair, "Mornin." *Damn it feels good to wake up with her in my arms.*

"Sorry I fell asleep." She whispered.

"It's okay. We had a long night." I lean my head into her and place a light kiss on her neck.

"It's going to be a huge day. Are you ready for the race?" She reminds me I am racing the sexiest car I've ever laid eyes on this evening.

"I've been ready for this my whole life. Besides, I'll have you by my side." I place my hand on her face and gently brush my thumb across her cheek in a sweeping motion.

"We have a lot to prepare for. If it runs good have you thought about doing a call out?" Atlanta places her hand on mine and lightly squeezes it and she smiles sweetly.

"You know I have always wanted to be on that list. I'm not going to get my hopes up that the car is already capable of that speed. It might need some extras, but to answer your question; yes I will do a call out." I push myself up with my elbows higher on the couch.

"I have a feeling today is your lucky day." She beams over at me before standing up and walking into the kitchen to start the coffee. She makes the cup and won't touch it for thirty minutes before she starts to drink it. She likes it cold. Oddball if you ask me. I don't drink the stuff though so I can't judge. I am all about that lime green liquid poison.

No matter what time of day I can't get enough. She grabs a bottle from the fridge tossing it at me. It's a good thing I played little league or I would have missed it. She bounces off to her room. Darn near a half a bottle later, I sit it down, forgotten once I get a glimpse of Atlanta brushing her hair. I can feel the long silly strands in my fingers and my temperature heats up to an almost boiling over degree.

It extends down to the end of her back and reaches the top of her jeans. She catches me watching her and smiles, her eyes twinkling. "Creeper!" She chuckles, disappearing back into the bathroom. When she comes out this time, she has her hair pulled back into a high messy bun showing off the small star tattoos just behind her left ear. Something about them drives me wild.

Standing up off the couch, I stand behind her, and run my thumb over the small stars then kiss her in the same spot. I notice goosebumps appear on her arms. I can also feel the need building in my pants. Before these emotions get the best of us and before we are ready for the next level, I turn to walk to the bathroom. After doing the morning routine, I meet her back in the living room. "I'm going to drive home, take care of some things, and take a cold shower." I smile slyly and kiss her softy.

She smirks, "I never knew I had this effect on you. I like it."

I open the front door. "See you in a couple hours."

On my way home all I can think about is, Wow what a night. I can't fathom all this stuff coming in my favor. All my life I have wanted a smoking car and Atlanta.

Two things I thought weren't in my reach and here they are front and center. This must be a dream. Life can't be this good. The cold shower will wake me up to reality I am sure. I pull into the drive of my small yellow mobile home. It is quaint, but it has a garage attached that holds all my valuables--Tools and more tools. Some, I bought myself and loads my parents and Ed have given me over the years. I pull the car into the garage, turn off the engine, and get out. I pop the hood and start checking every hose, bolt and fluid. I need her to be completely ready for tonight. Only practicing a couple times, I don't want something to happen to make the car look bad for the old man. Everything looks good and my gas is around a quarter of a tank which is perfect since I need the car to be light for the race. My phone chimes and I tug it out of my pocket not remembering the grease on my hands. Damn. I rub it against my shirt and look to see who it is.

CAMRY: What time will you be at the track?

Me: Nine sharp. Race starts at ten.

CAMRY: Okay. How's the car handling?

Me: Smooth

CAMRY: Sweet! See you at 10.

I slide the phone back in my pocket. I finish checking out the car and change the street tires to slicks. It's dark so the cops won't notice and since I don't have a trailer for the car yet, I have to chance it getting to the track without tire damage or being pulled over. The race tonight is street-legal since it's at the track.

The rules are simple and there is no chance for the law getting on your case about your speed, but they do stand guard to watch for the dumb racers that can't handle losing and get out of control. Now, my real passion is for the street. The rush that comes when you are on a straight dark road and you burn out with cops hiding in in the bushes waiting to bust someone. That's a thrill. I should have been a NASCAR driver so I could drive maxed out on the track. Who am I ragging? I like the aspect of every driver for himself or herself. This way I can know without a doubt if I am any good or not. I've never won, but I plan on winning in this car. I have a feeling about her and it's time for a win with my girl by my side. Speaking of her, I grab my phone out of my pocket and send her a quick text.

Me: Hey, sugar. I was just thinking about tomorrow night. We should order some flowers for Dani and have them delivered. Will you call and order them since you are better at that then me? You can have Yanair at the florist bill me.

Atlanta: Men, can't you do anything without a woman? JK & yes I will. Great idea.

Me: Counting down till I see you again. 45 mins to go.

Atlanta: I might make you wait a little longer when you come pick me up.

Me: I'm 100% you are worth it

Atlanta: You know it.

Me: Duh!

I pick up the mess, stroll to the back porch of my house, take a seat on the steps, unlace the strings, and slip the boots off placing them on the top step then dig in my front jeans pocket for my house keys. Grabbing my keys, and unlock the back door. I empty the contents of my pockets on the kitchen counter before walking to the master bathroom and slide open the plain navy blue shower curtain and turn the water to my liking. I strip down and drop my dirty clothes into the white wicker hamper to the left of the sink.

After my shower, I get dressed in some dark jeans, my cowboy boots, and an orange Dukes t-shirt. I style my mess of a fro into the usual shaggy do and slip on my lucky Ford ball cap. It has been with me since the day I won my first go cart race against little Mike Shaffer in the sixth grade. I had spent every weekend for the entire summer trying to beat him, but never succeeded until that night and after that he never won against me again. I haven't seen him since we graduated. Last, I heard he works Knoxville at a large customs shop that pimps rides out for famous people. I think I even heard about a TV show in the works for them. It would be cool to see what kind of stuff that they do to the cars. I could get some ideas to use at Edwards. It's it time to drive to get Atlanta. I send her a short text.

Me: On my way.

I do a one over on the car and shake my head before I get in the driver's seat and do ninety, okay more like thirty-five on these city streets to Atlanta's apartment. I can't remember when she ever had the same appearance longer than two days and today is no different.

She bounces down the flight of old wooden stairs with her strangest look yet. Multi-colored eyebrows. That's right they match her hair color filled with royal blue, lavender and pink with a touch of brown blended in. I crinkle my nose at her. She doesn't let the unsure look on my face take away from the fact she proud of being unique.

"What, rainbow brows aren't your thing?" She nudges my shoulder before climbing in the passenger window Hazzard style. She is so hot in her cut off shorts and a black Fancy Mafia t-shirt that has a gun made out to be a deer on the front. The antlers are encrusted with rhinestones that sparkle with every slight movement.

"Sugar, you are my thing and if that means I'm coloring rainbows and riding ponies then I suppose that's what I'll do." I open the car door and slide into the driver's seat, turning the key and close my eyes for a split second to take in the roar of the beast.

"Speaking of ponies. The fair is here this week and I am dying to go. Wanna be my date? She tilts her head towards me and bats her beautiful blue eyes.

"Of course, just tell me when you want to go." I answer as I pull the gearshift into reverse.

"Also…" She peers up at me. I can't help but smile because I know for the rest of our lives I'll do anything that makes her smile. "Dani is going to have a booth there and I… Umm…kind of told her we would help and make cotton candy. You in?" She beams showing her pearly whites so much that I can't focus on backing up the car.

I put the car in first gear and begin driving, "Is that why you look like cotton candy?" I can't help but let out a loud laugh.

"Make fun, but at least I try new things. I mean…haven't you had that shirt since you were like twelve." She pinches the fabric between her fingers and tugs on it. Her playfulness is so enduring and hot. She has the spirit of the young girl I met in daycare, but also the womanly attitude she has grown into.

I don't even have to agree to the fair booth because she knows it's a given I will be there. Following her as I always do and always will. I'm not embarrassed, it's just the facts and that's okay. Some men are born to follow their woman and bow at their feet and some women are born to do the same. It's how we handle our role in the process which creates our characters. I have followed, but I still have a life of my own. Sure, it's small in comparison to hers, but if I sat back and thought about how I would want to live my life, I would be exactly where I am right now. Completely driven by the fast cars and the fast woman I have loved since I could tie my own shoelaces.

5

Dinks

I pull my car onto the track and line it up to the starting line. We have the first race of the evening and it's a good thing, because I'm not sure how long the old man will hold up out here in this crowd. Atlanta opens her door and gets out before I shut the car off. She is overly excited because Dani came to watch and those two are peas in a pod. Dani runs over and the two of them hug like they just saw each other for the first time after an extended absence and I know they were together for lunch while I went home to clean up. Dani is sporting black hair with pink strands today. I step out of the car after shutting the engine off and close the door. I hear a strong sweet voice behind me and turn to see who it is.

"Dare." Her blonde hair swings inward around her face when the wind blows and she trucks it behind her ears. "This is my father Frank Grant. I thought you should meet before you race his baby." Camry introduces her dad to me. "Hi Sir, it is very nice to meet you. I can't get over the beauty you have built. She is one of a kind." I exclaim and pat the top of the car with my hand.

He just looks at me and doesn't say anything. I can see the illness in his eyes and the stillness of his body. I know if I was in his place I would be smiling on the inside and from what I googled on the disease that is what it leads too.

"I'll do my best sir to make you proud." Camry throws her arms around my neck and hugs me. I hug her back feeling a little emotional with the situation. I look up and notice Atlanta watching me. I smile at her to try and ease her worries and she smiles back. I don't know if she is jealous but I think I'd like it if she was. Just knowing she would care enough to be concerned for the slightest second is kind of hot.

Camry releases her grip and grabs my hand in hers. "Thank you again for doing this. I know you get to keep the car but I know that you wouldn't be taking it if I weren't making you. You're a good guy, I can see it." She tightens her grip.

"You can change your mind at any moment. As much as I want the pink slip, I'm okay with giving it back." I admit letting her hand slip from mine.

"Time for me to go meet the other drivers for tonight." I inform her before walking off to the lineup.

The drivers are shouting their call outs for the race and I walk over to the lead director Wade Burkes and explain the situation and he agrees to race me without ever seeing the car run. This could get me on the list of fastest cars at number ten or it could just show Mr. Grant the baby he built can stand against the fastest cars in the state. I won't let him down either way. No last place for this beast.

I observe Camry staring at me a lot tonight. She is a really pretty and caring girl. Not many around that fit both categories anymore. These days if they have good looks then they know it and act as if they are more relevant than anyone else. It's nice to meet another one of the good ones. Atlanta and Dani are a couple others in the same group. I have yet to date a girl that is genuine until now.

Atlanta would do this for her dad if she was in the same situation and that makes my heart ache for Camry. I can picture it being Atlanta and I would hate to see her with so much pain. Camry has held herself together around me, but I notice the pain in her eyes and the stress around them when she talks about him. She is much too young to handle things on her own and even though we are around the same age, I feel somewhat responsible for her happiness. I smile up at her before turning back to the leader.

The run is about to start and I can feel my blood pressure boiling close to the surface with every easing minute. Time slows. I am so anxious and silence is louder than the roaring engines. I hear boot heels getting closer to me. I turn and lay eyes on my love. The one reason my life has always had meaning, "Hey sugar." I beam.

"Do I need to worry about blondie?" She dead faces me.

"In all the years we have been friends you have never had to worry about any other woman. It's always been you" I assure her, slinging my arm over her shoulder and pulling her into my chest. "It could be because of your ever changing looks that you always feel like a different woman." I tease, but not well.

She pulls away from me and punches me hard in the upper arm. "Just like a man." She smirks.

I grab my arm in pain. "Careful sugar, I need this arm to drive." I rub it for relief. "Please I didn't hit you that hard sissy." She crinkles her adorable nose. "So...sissy, are you ready to win this race and get the pink?" Atlanta asks while she rubs my wounded arm.

"Ready, but scared I won't do the car justice." I admit.

"How could you not when you have so much passion in your heart for the car and so much empathy for Mr. Grant. You will do amazing and I will be on the sidelines cheering you on." Her hand slides down to mine and she gently squeezes it. I give her a confused look.

"You aren't riding with me?" I ask.

"No. I have always seen the way you hold back when I am shotgun. The other night I wasn't and you flew." Atlanta leans in and kisses my cheek.

I can't help but fall harder for her. She always knows the exact thing I need to focus. Right now, I need to only concentrate on the race and later the good Lord willing, I can only think about her. She kisses me lightly, turns on her heels, and walks off toward the finish line. I pause and stand there with my lower lip slightly dropped as I watch her walk away. She is tiny framed but still has curves and the rear is a little fuller than most girls her size. Plump and perfect. I'm not even sure if we are ready for that part of the relationship to change. I still need to get used to the idea that she wants me as more than her best friend but I want all of her. Every inch.

I stroll over to the car and Camry is at my side. "Thanks again. I'll see you at the finish line." She pushes her dad down the track where the crowd is waiting.

I shake the hand of my competition and we both get in our cars. Seat belts buckled and helmets on.

After a deadly race a few months ago, where one of the drivers died from a head injury we are now required to wear helmets. Frankly, it is smart to be required. Most of us wouldn't wear them because it doesn't look manly enough. I mean let's face it. Racing is for the coolest of people and a helmet makes it more of a kid's game instead of a race for men.

Personally, I would rather look like a wimp than chance a head injury I can't recover from. That being said, Atlanta would kick my butt if I didn't protect myself.

The flag girl gives us the signal to start our engines. The beast next to me roars under the engine. I can feel the vibrations all the way over here in my car. It's hot as heck. I turn the key in the ignition and the motor is strong. I close my eyes and listen for anything that might sound off, but I hear nothing. I take in a deep breath and open my eyes. Down the long stretch of asphalt, I can see her orange shirt stand out from the crowd. That's where I am headed as fast as I can. To her. She is my finish line. I shake off all the distractions and concentrate only on the car and the road. I let the girl know I am ready by giving the standard thumbs up. When she nods, I grip the sterling wheel tight with one hand and clinch the gearshift in the other. The flag drops and I sling the handle into first gear then quickly into second, third and fourth before we get halfway down the track. The car next to me is a bumper ahead of me, but I drop it down to fifth and the car takes on a life of its own. I inch up closer and at this point in the race, we are side by side.

I focus on the feeling the car is giving me, but the rush of adrenaline takes over my senses, I lose focus on what I am doing, and for one second I ease of the gas. It is too late to get the edge on him, but I do end up so close that we are only a foot apart when we cross the finish line.

I put the car in park and lean my head back on the headrest and inhale. I can't believe I just raced one of the fastest cars in the state and nearly beat him. This car is badass. I can't help but smile. Heck, I'm sure my face is going to be twisted into this dumb look for the rest of my life. I don't know what I did to deserve to get both my dreams at once but damn I'm glad I am.

Someone opening the driver's side door startles me. Atlanta screams, "Oh my God this car is fast as hell and Dare, you did it. Sure, you didn't win but let's be real your competition wasn't that much ahead of you. If you did it again I know you would have him looking like he switched gears to reverse." She is straddling my lap by now and her already short shorts have now disappeared under her orange t-shirt. I put one hand on her thigh and the other one the side of her face. I am still in shock that the car pulled off the impossible, but feeling her skin next to mine and smelling her soft clean scent relaxes me. All I can see or think about is her and feeling her closer to me and never letting her go. I stare into her eyes and kiss her hard. It doesn't register to be gentle or to savor the moment. Right now, all I want is to have my way with her and pronto.

She isn't the best friend that I have loved my whole life but instead she is the lover that turns me into the madly spontaneous man that doesn't care that we are on a racetrack with hundreds of people waiting for me to get out of the car.

After what seems like hours, we get out of the car and I am greeted with the leader Wade. "I guess you can count yourself number eleven on my list. Once your head lands back on the ground call me and I will go over the rules and when the next race is going to be."

I shake his hand and still grinning like a kid that just did something sneaky. "Thanks man." I manage to get two words out. As Wade saunters off, I notice Camry pushing Mr. Grant closer to me in his wheelchair. I grab Atlanta's hand and we start walking to meet them. I lean down, place my hand on his arm, and gaze into his deep green eyes. He can't speak or make any motions that he is in his body but I know he is. I know he saw his car cross the finish line and his dream came true. I take great pleasure in knowing I could do something for someone in this situation or any other one.

"You have built one fast car sir and I would bet money it is number one before you know it. Just need to work on the driver, that's all." I assure him before standing. Camry hugs me again. Atlanta's face is priceless. I have never seen her jealous side before and I am not sure why she is showing it now but it's cute. Camry slips a piece of paper into my hand without anyone noticing but I am curious to what it is so I gaze down and see it is the title to the car. "You know you don't have to do this. It was a pleasure to drive it and I don't expect you to really give me the…" She puts the tips of her fingers over my lips. "He doesn't know." My eyes get large by her confession. "I'll tell him later. Thank you again." She continues.

I tuck the folded title into my back pocket and nod my head. I am rushed with girls squealing my name and boys yanking on me like a rope in tug of war. I am not one for this kind of attention and am starting to wig out a little. This is Atlanta's thing, not mine. She notices how uncomfortable I am and quickly comes to my rescue. I watch her intently as she slides her thumb and index finger into the corners of her lips and lets out this gut wrenching whistle. The crowd goes silent and stares in her direction, only a few steps from me.

"Excuse me for a moment while I congratulate my boyfriend on his run." Her blue eyes scan over the crowd as she makes her way to me. "Everyone get in line. Dare, can talk to you one by one." She informs them before planting a big kiss on me. I lose myself in the moment and forget about the several dozen people waiting to talk to me. Her lips taste like vanilla and strawberry and her skin feels like silk when I rub my fingertips along her cheek. Every time we kiss, it feels like the first time.

The first glorious time she became mine, and I became hers. The best day of my life to date, and that includes today with the pink slip to the challenger tucked in my back pocket.

6

Art Queen

Last night was so full of adrenaline I am looking forward to a quiet evening with friends. Dani is one of our best friends and after everything she went through with her mom, she deserves to have some happy just for her. I'm excited to see the beauty she has created in the form of art. Not many country bumpkins appreciate the arts, but for me it is like classic cars and beautiful women. Rare and one of a kind. I have seen her passion for art since we were in high school. Every week she created a new piece and blew us away with her talents. I haven't seen anything she couldn't take on and master.

"Sugar, are you ready yet? We are going to be late and you know Dani has a stomach full of butterflies without you." I shout out toward Atlanta's bedroom.

I am turned toward the television watching the news when I hear her whisper, "I'm ready" I turn in her direction. My mouth hits the floor. She looks hot. I mean stainless steel gas grill hot.

Atlanta is wearing a simple black fitted dress, black heels, and a turquoise beaded necklace. It's elegant without the flash most women would wear. Her tattoos are a lot like jewelry and make a statement on their own.

I love each one, and I catch myself thinking about the story behind them. Each piece holds a special meaning right down to the common rose or the Marilyn image.

I stand up and walk over to her. "You look beautiful."

"Thank you. We better get going. Don't want Dani's butterflies to take over her body, do you?" She grabs her phone off the kitchen counter and strolls to the door. She always does this. I'll wait for her until we are nearly late and she will come out, stand by the door with her hand on her hip, and act like she has been waiting on me the whole time. So damn cute.

I reach and pick up my keys on the small table next to the door and then turn the golden knob and hold the door open for her to walk through first since I am a gentleman. Mainly, because I want to watch her walk down the stairs in that sexy dress. It's very elegant but I am a guy, so I'm going to look, and I'm going to look a lot. Her long legs take each step carefully in the heels, careful not to fall. I lock the door and follow her down. When we reach the bottom step she trips and stumbles backward toward me. I catch her one-handed gripping her ass. Best excuse without actually having to create one. Sometimes accidents are meant to be and this was all in my favor.

The building is in the downtown Nashville Art District. It is a blue two-story building with wrought iron tables outside the front and a huge window with wrought-iron shutters on the second floor. During the lunch rush, she told us a hot dog vender sits out front so she thought she would add tables for people to sit at and enjoy the few moments away from their hectic workday.

I wouldn't be surprised if she didn't bring them blankets on the days it is cold or water on the hot days. She is the type that mothers those around her and makes you feel all warm and fuzzy like when you were a child with your parents. Atlanta always calls her when she is sick because she will pamper her and it speeds up the healing process she says. Honestly, I think Atlanta just says that so she can have homemade dumplings and sour cream pound cake. I have to admit her pound cake is out of this world and I'm secretly hope Dani made some for tonight's event. It's been a few weeks since Atlanta had a brush with pollen and called Dani on the phone pouting about her clogged up sinuses. I know Dani has caught on and eats it up that Atlanta needs her.

I park a half a block away on the street and turn the ignition off. It has been nearly twenty-four hours since this car was officially mine. I meant to call and see how Camry was doing, but today was spent with my first love and we haven't had many days together since we announced our love at the bar the other night. I will have to call her tomorrow during a break from work. Now, tonight is all about the beauty next to me. We both get out of the car and even though I would really like to open her door for her, I know she is independent and the last time I did that she didn't let me live it down. She doesn't want things to change completely between us and I don't blame her. The friendship we have is one of a kind and we need to remember that before the romantic relationship we are trying to build. She reaches for my hand as we are walking to the gallery and I entwine my fingers into hers. Her temperature is so warm it heats my body. I can see already this is going to be a long night. That heat, those heels, and that damn short skirt are going to be the only things my body can focus on.

I have been to the gallery many times before tonight, to help with the miscellaneous items such as painting the walls and changing light fixtures. That is one reason friends are awesome to have around. Their skills. The front of the building is simple, but through the clear glass windows, the room is filled with people in evening attire and exquisite art. Dani's eighteen-year-old cousin Nicole that I call Nico greets us at the door. She has a tiny girl crush on me and I cannot help but encourage it out of pure fun and let's be real, it helps my ego a little. I know she is just nearly past jailbait but it does inflate a man's ego some to know I still got it with the ladies. Besides, unless you are blind like Atlanta you can see I only have eyes for one lady.

"Hi Nico, how have you been?" I wrap my arms around her and pull her in for a hug. She giggles and places her small hand on my back. "I've been good. School is boring but I'll live. Dani gave me a job here after school and I'm really pumped about it. She is going places you know." She beams up at me. I release her from my grasp and grab Atlanta's hand. "Oh my God! You two are a couple now. When did this happen?" Nico glances at me and then back to Atlanta.

"It hasn't been a week yet, but it feels like a lifetime." I state, in awe of Atlanta.

"It's good to know you both came to your senses. The rest of us have been waiting for this to happen. We just thought you two were two souls that would never connect." Nico lips curl into a smile.

"I better get back to work. Dani is in the back with a big buyer." She continues before strolling back to the front door.

Dani is in her element tonight. She is dressed in a long pink lace dress with white heels. It goes perfectly with her hair color for the day. Blonde with light pink stripes. That is something Atlanta and her have in common. The ever-changing hair color. Still holding Atlanta's hand I tug her a little closer and her body lines with mine. It's like Cupid finally hit us both with the correct love arrow and now our souls have connected. She fits perfectly by my side. Unlike most couples, we have one up on them. We started as friends first and now, since we know the annoying habits the other has we can move on to the good stuff like relaxing our wall, enjoy each other's company, and build a relationship that will last forever. The fun has just begun and I am treasuring every second.

Atlanta pulls away, runs up to Dani and gives her a huge hug when we reach her. "Babe, everything looks so wonderful."

Dani hugs her back tightly, "Let me walk you both around and show you all the exhibits."

Dani clasps Atlanta's hand and mine and walks in between us around to each separate wall that displays a collection as we admire the different pieces. Her work is truly breathtaking. In the center of each different series of art, there is a sculpture on a pillar standing completely alone. It is simple, yet it draws you in and fills the entire collection as a whole.

After an exquisite music collection featuring a painting of a young child on a toy piano, we round the corner for the last collection she has on display. Atlanta and I stare at the stunning photographs and paintings that cover the entire wall. "This is the soulmate collection." Dani squeezes our hands tightly before placing them together. "It's about time they finally came together." I gasp and turn back to the wall. The pieces are a timeline of my and Atlanta's life. It starts with a painting of two young children playing on a jungle gym and ends with a photograph of Atlanta and myself dancing at a concert a few months back. We were both so happy and very unaware of anyone around us, which seems to happen a lot. The center sculpture is two different sets of hands with the fingers entwined together. The closer I look, I can see that they are ours. The side of the female hand has a small heart located on the wrist near the thumb. I rub Atlanta's wrist with my finger. "This is beyond beautiful…I'm speechless." Atlanta's voice is soft and airy. "How did you manage to keep this hidden?" I ask.

"It was hard but, I kept it at my house in the spare bedroom under a few sheets in case you surprised me and walked in one day. Lucky for me, neither of you did," Dani informs us.

I turn and release Atlanta's hand so I can hug Dani. She hugs back and Atlanta joins us wrapping her long arms around us both. I'm sure all the clients in the room have started to focus on us and all the attention we are getting from the star of the evening, but its okay. I can handle a few stares.

"I have to have one of these Dani." I inform her. She bites her upper lip and leans her head down to the wood floor.

"Well you see…they are sold. An anonymous buyer bought each one and I was just handed the invoice before walking you both over here. My first sale!" She unfolds a small yellow paper and hands it to me. I hold the pale paper in my hands and see the price of the artwork.

"Dang girl, I couldn't have afforded them anyway. I'm so proud of you." I wrap my arms around her again.

"Wait for me." Atlanta encloses her thin arms around both of us. "I'm excited. Where's the wine?" She continues loosening her grip. Dani points to the bar and Atlanta disappears out of our line of vision.

"I wonder why the buyer wants to be anonymous. Kind of creepy, ya think?" I step a few steps back and admire the art collection some more.

"I'm not sure. Maybe they didn't want to make a big deal of it since it was the first sale of the night." Dani hits my shoulder with hers.

Maybe she is right and the buyer is on the shy side and doesn't want to make a big thing out of the sale. I would want everyone to know I could afford to buy something so expensive and breathtaking. Let's be real though. I would never want to be the guy that wants people to see him for the money. I want people to see me as they see my grandfather; strong, independent, caring, and hard working. He was one of a kind with a genuine soul. People all around would flock to him for any reason they wanted and they knew that he would lend a hand or an ear if they needed it.

Atlanta glides back over to Dani and me carrying three glasses of champagne. We take ours, I raise mine for a toast, and their glasses follow suit. "To Dani, for making her dream come true and having the ability to create such stunning masterpieces.

Here's too many more." I say. The sound of our clinking glasses echo in the spacious room. Dani excuses herself to go mingle with the other guests. Atlanta and I stand in silence for what feels likes the rest of the evening, but couldn't have been more than a few minutes. I clasp her hand in mine. "You are so beautiful. The photographs here are moments I have etched in my brain. Here you are in the small garage of Alex's house." I point to one of the photographs hanging on the wall. "This was the first band practice for you and the freaks. I remember thinking this would be it for me. You would become a famous singer and I would never see you again. Who would have known I would go with you to every concert?" I stand silent again.

"I always knew I would want you at every step." She said before she kissed me.

"This photo is right after I realized I loved you. See my eyes when I'm looking at you. I can see the love in them. I was so afraid of messing things up after so many failed relationships. I was blind. I never thought for a minute you would love me too or that you felt this way for so many years." Atlanta turns and faces me. I slip my noticeably working hands on either side of her face and lean in for a kiss. It starts soft and slow and begins to pick up pace. "We should get out of here." I whisper between breaths.

7
All Mine

We leave the gallery in a rush. I don't know what happened, but the uncomfortable and weird emotions release and filled with a ton of passion. My body's temperature builds with every hard breath I take. I love this woman and I need to be with her now. I can't stop staring over at her. Keeping my eyes on the road is hard as hell with the growing desire filling my pants. My palms are sweaty and I try to rub them on my pants while discreetly rubbing around my zipper to tame the beast that has awoken. Damn the drive back to her apartment feels like an eternity when it is only minutes. Atlanta's breathing is sharp and quick which makes my body rage with emotion deep in my pants. I wrench the car into her back lot and turn off the engine. We both open the car doors at the same time and pace fast inside the upstairs apartment. Atlanta tosses her house key on the counter and I shove mine in my front pocket. Here we are two best friends about to become lovers. There is no question from either of us. The heat roars and the tension has vanished. I don't hold anything back anymore.

"I love you Atlanta. I really love you." I whisper before surrounding my trembling lips on hers. We stumble back into her bedroom and hastily remove our own clothes and drop them where we stand. Her body is smooth like silk and she smells of vanilla and peony.

I can't get enough and I tug her body closer to mine and slowly lay her on the bed. Her hair falls around her face and I pause to take her in. I want to see the entire sight of her in this moment. I lean down, placing my face near her ear and take in a deep breath. I can smell her essence and it fills my senses, overtaking me and my body begins to move slowly against hers.

"God, you are beautiful." I breathe.

"You aren't so bad yourself, handsome." She entangles her fingers in my messy copper hair, and with a slight yank, our lips meet again.

I want to take my time and burn into my memory what is transpiring between us but I can't. I need to release the burning inside me.

She must feel the same, because she rolls me over and straddles me. Her long hair falls onto my stomach and tickles my skin creating goosebumps where it touches.

"I love you, Dare." She murmurs.

The power of her words send me into overdrive. I press myself deep inside her and we both release the pressure that has been building and the love we have been holding back.

The night couldn't have been more perfect. For a man, I always thought women over dramatized making love when it was just sex. Sex has always been the same with every girl I have been with-- until now. I would get mine and they would get theirs. There weren't any feelings other than that. Tonight proved me wrong. Making love is so much better than anyone can describe.

I'm pretty much ruined for life now, so Atlanta had better never leave me. I'd be screwed or should I say unscrewed for life. We are both still naked lying in bed. Normally this would be where I would get up and leave, but I am not going anywhere. She will have to throw me out. I wrap my muscular arms around her small body and pull her into me. The scent of vanilla and peonies fill the room and overpowers the normal incense smell. I'll never be able to go a day without smelling her. I am complete. She has filled my heart and now in this moment I have everything a man could ever want. "Thank you." I whisper.

"For what?" She asks gently squeezing my hand in hers.

"For loving me back. You have always been my cloud nine and now I have it all. My life is complete," I croon.

She turns her body to face me. "I don't know why I never saw it. I know it was there. It had to be, but what I don't know is why I was so clueless to it. This feels so natural to me." She leans up and kisses my lips.

"We don't need to worry about the past anymore. Now the only thing that matters is the future-- a long happy one together."

I never dreamt I would be where I am today. In this bed with her. My dream car sitting outside. If I didn't know better I would think I was dreaming. Atlanta dozes off and I lie watching her breathe in and out. She makes the cutest sounds while she sleeps. A cross between a kitten's purr and a bird's chirp.

It's enough to put me to sleep, but I strain to keep my eyes open for as long as I can to take in every second I can with her, like this. Our worlds have changed and mine has just begun.

I am light headed from the world wind of today's release and a little nervous about tomorrow but one thing is certain… I am content and floating on air.

I wake up before Atlanta so I am still not to rouse her, but I can't resist the perfect pout her lips are making. I lean down and slowly press my lips to hers. As if it is an instinct she kisses mine back. Our lips move together as one and her eyes open. We gaze at each other with so much love that I can't take my eyes from her. Atlanta stretches herself outward towards the bed, away from me, she giggles, and she says, "I think I had the best night sleep ever." I can't help but smile.

She is so breathtakingly beautiful in the morning. Everything is well...perfect! "So what's our plan today?" Atlanta asks while clutching my hair and twirling it between her fingers.

"Well, I think that we should probably see if Dani needs any help cleaning her studio today since we did leave early. Then, I thought maybe we could go for a drive to the lake."

"Which car are we gonna take? Yours or mine?" She smirks.

"I did just get mine and I'm ready to put some wear and tear on those fat tires." I confess.

I get out of bed, stretch, and walk into the bathroom to brush my teeth and get ready for the day. From where I am standing I watch Atlanta roll over spreading out all across the bed; hogging the entire thing. Once I am finished cleaning up, I walk back into the bedroom and she is still just lying in the bed. I quickly turn my head away from her as an instinct when she sits up and the cover falls to her lap. "Dare, you've seen it all now." She laughs.

I jump on the bed and straddle her slender legs. "It's going to take some getting used to, but only the things that are habit. Trust me when I say that will be the last time I try to shield my eyes."

"It better be." She states before I press my lips into hers.

I slide my body hastily off hers and advise her to get up and get ready while I go make breakfast and text Dani.

I pick up my phone from the table where I left it last night near her bed and I send a quick text to Dani.

Me: Do you need any help today?

Dani: I hired someone to clean up. I'm not even there right now.

Me: Ok. You rocked it last night. Atlanta and I are still bummed we didn't get to purchase a piece.

Dani: I'm sure I can whip you guys up something for perhaps…a wedding.

Me: Woah. Slow down. We just started dating.

Dani: You both have been dating your whole lives. Now it's time to speed things up before one of you go stupid again.

Me: I'll see what I can do, Mom!

Dani: Lol.

Atlanta steps out of the bedroom and is wearing a bright green towel, her hair is dripping wet, and mascara has surrounds her eyes. The smell of French toast and sugary syrup I just removed from the microwave fill the air. Atlanta sits on the bar stool taking in a deep breath. "I love you." She mutters. The words reach deep inside me and warm it like the first bite of the French toast.

I stop and study her, "I love you too."

I pour the warm liquid over the toast and lightly sprinkle it with confectioners' sugar and cinnamon. I slide the plate over to her and hand her a fork. I work on my plate next then take a seat beside her once it's made.

She cuts a piece and pokes it with her fork before slipping it in her mouth. A small drop of syrup drips on her chin. I smile. "Do you want me to get that for you?"

She laughs. "You better."

I lean into her and slowly lick the drop off and kiss her. I progress gradually up to her lips. The taste of her and the sugar makes me crazy. A deep hum sound irrupts from my throat. I don't want our relationship to be just about sex, but let's be honest this has been building for years. I pull away and take a bite of my food. She gazes at me out of the corner of her eye. "Now, I know what I love about your ass. It's the cooking." She teases.

After breakfast, we wash up the dishes and wipe down the counter. I sit on the couch and play a racing game while she saunters off to get dressed.

I am so into the game that I don't notice what is going on in the apartment but once I hear her shout from the bedroom my attention focuses on the doorway. "You think this is okay for a picnic?"

Atlanta steps out of her room wearing black yoga pants, a green low cut tank top, and black tennis shoes. "Oh my…yes." I choke on the words a little as I recall the night before and take in how hot she looks right now. "We could just stay in." I tease.

She grabs a jacket off the back of her chair which lets me know she is ready. "We could, but I'm ready now and my heart is set on the lake."

I chuckle, stand and make my way to the door, locking it behind us. Once we are in the Challenger, I rest the bag I packed in the back seat. I crank the car and I get slightly enthusiastic. I love feeling the power it has under me. Atlanta can see the eagerness on my face and she beams at me. Little does she know, it's her smile I love more than anything.

I back out of the back lot and pull onto the road. The mornings are peaceful around here since the concerts and performances usually happen in the evening. Nashville has many twists and turns, which leave very little need for speed, however there is an exceedingly long road we use for street racing from time to time, and once we get to it, I can't help but floor it.

My baby is so fast that one would wonder if she could fly. Atlanta spends the entire way to the lake listening to eighties rock. I'm sure that material girl was on repeat. I love and respect all music, but what guy wants to listen to "like a virgin" all day long. We pull into the campsite area and I park the car and shut off the engine. A sigh of relief rushes over me not to have to listen to that for at least five minutes if I'm lucky. I grab the bag from the back and reach for Atlanta's hand. She takes mine and we walk down to the shoreline. She releases my hand and lays out a blue flannel blanket. I sit the bag on top of it to keep the wind from blowing it away. We both plop down and scoot close together. I can smell her vanilla and peony scent every time the wind blows. I breathe it in. I breathe her in.

Call Out

My phone vibrates. I slip my hand in the front of my jeans pocket and slide it out. Once I see the text, I say it aloud so Atlanta knows who it is. Wade!

WADE: You busy?

ME: Hey man, what's up?

WADE: That race was bad ass dude. You killed it!

I'm not surprised he raves about the race since the car is so dang awesome but, it's nice hearing it from someone with the fastest car in the state. Wade owns a handful of classic muscle cars. The race the other night wasn't one of his fastest but, it is the top five in the state. On a list of ten, he owns two of the spots. His metallic gold, 1970 Chevelle is number one out of everyone in the state of Tennessee and it holds the number four spot nationwide. He might be five-six in stature, but his car knowledge and street racing skills have made him a legend.

WADE: I am planning a race and thought I would give you the option to call out the number ten spot. I don't think you should wait any longer.

I turn to Atlanta who is reading over my shoulder. "What are you waiting for? This has been your dream since we were kids." She nudges me then leans into my lips and kisses me tenderly.

ME: Let's do this. I call out number ten.

I am a little nervous as I type out the words. My hands are trembling. Sure, Atlanta and I have raced each other before but that was playing around. This is the real deal. The races at the track have nothing on a full-blown call out. Street racing is for hard-core racers. They know to max out every inch of their beast and push it beyond the limit and that's going to be me. Oh shit, that's going to be me. What am I thinking? Adding this to my list of dreams come true. I have it all right now and I am terrified because for so long I didn't have any of it. It makes me wonder how much life I have left after I have it all. What do you do when all your dreams have come true? Surely, I can come up with more goals and create more dreams, but isn't a dream something you fantasize about instead of something you make up?

Atlanta squeals and brings a smile to my face. Wade agrees to do the call out and she sees the text before I can focus my eyes on the screen. I have one week to plan, train and figure out the car I have only driven a handful of times. I have to get over my fear of not making it and letting off the gas just before crossing the finish line.

Something I do at the track. Something always holds me back and won't let me keep going, and every time I fail.

Atlanta bounces with excitement, she jumps towards me, I fall backwards on the blanket, and she lands on top of me. With slow kisses, she ravishes my mouth. We lay there in a make out session for quite a while and after years of waiting for days like these; I am certainly not going to rush it.

We spend the rest of the day at the lake and watch the sunset. It's perfect like her. Maybe this will be my new dream. More days like this, an entire life with her and possibly a family together. Heck, I already have a third of the dream so now I just need to fill in the pieces.

The following evening begins our four-night favor to Dani. We are going to manage the cotton candy booth for her so she can take a break. It doesn't sound like a lot of work but in all honesty, I want to prepare my car for the weekend. Friends come first and it's only for a couple hours. Atlanta of course is excited. She has this thing for carnival rides. The Extreme ride to be exact, and I'm not too fond of it. She has always been one for the high flying fast and furious rides and I prefer the ground of the floorboard as the case may be.

She looks so dang hot in her light denim button up shorts and a dark purple tank top with the words, 'I like it sticky'. Perfect quote since we are manning the cotton candy booth. Her hair is just the way I like it with her natural dark chestnut, but she added in a few highlights of purple in it. There is something about her natural color I love the most. I don't know if it is because I watched her grow up with this shade, or because the other colors wash her away. This one just shows her. The true beauty of Atlanta Lane Reed.

I am wearing my usual ragged out blue jeans and a basic concert tee. You know 'AC/DC rocks' and let's face it everyone should have one.

We take Atlanta's mustang and give my car a rest. She insists on driving not to mention showing off some with a spin out in the parking lot. The overcrowded street is full of people that take notice at the squealing tires and smoke a few feet away from them. The girls turn and look with disgust spread on their faces while the men hoot and holler at the hot chick burning rubber. I can't blame them. It is sexy as hell.

We pull into the fair grounds and park. Once we get out, Atlanta stops and takes in the fair. It is starting to get dark and we start to see the lights glistening around the rides. One of the best things about her is that she does something most people forget-- to enjoy everything around you. She doesn't ignore the things that pass her, but instead embraces it. We have been to the fair a zillion times, but there she is seeing it like it is the first time.

We pay our entrance fee, and head back to the brown brick building in the back of the lot. There are several booths lined in rows featuring voting booths to art booths from local schools. Dani's booth is in the back corner of the building. All I can think about is what a bad idea this is. Two newly together people should not be in an under lit corner by themselves. Dani hugs us, and explains what steps to take in making the sugar floss and hands over a stack of cards to pass out for her gallery before leaving.

Atlanta and I look at each other in fear when we notice the line of kids waiting for the free cotton candy. Of course the kids from the entire town are here getting free floss since the stuff at the fair is five to six dollars a bag. All kids love sugar and parents love anything free.

Dani went above and beyond for the booth and has not only the common pink vanilla and blue raspberry flavors but she also has chocolate, coconut, lemon, and grape. Cotton candy flies and lands all over us. We are covered head to toe in sugar. Atlanta leans over and whispers in my ear, "Don't even think about it. You aren't licking this off me. There are kids around," I respond. "Buzz kill." She giggles. I notice the line has vanished and gaze over at her curious. She shrugs her shoulders. "Maybe they went to see the hypnotist act."

She pulls out the strawberry, makes herself a cone, and then adds the chocolate on top. She takes her fingers, pinches off a small piece of floss, and slides her eyes over in my direction. I notice her in the corner of my eye and I turn to watch. She slips her finger and piece of brown and pink floss in her mouth. Her lips close around her finger, and she pulls it slowly out.

Wow. I can't help but stand and stare. My mouth has hit the floor by now, going dry and other parts of me have stood up. I can't take my eyes off her as she repeats it again, one bite at a time. I stroll over to her, grasp her arm, and pull her finger into my mouth. I see her breath hitch as I slowly lick her finger and let every, last drop of sugar dissolve in my mouth. We both stare into each other's eyes when there is a loud Ahhum sound. We both turn and notice Dani standing there watching us. "Do you two need to go home or do you both want to put on a show?" Atlanta smiles and her cheeks flush. She is so embarrassed, and it is adorable. I start laughing hard. "If you want a show, we can do that, but if you are done with us then we can go home."

"Please go home." Dani laughs and rolls her eyes.

We gather our stuff and begin to leave. Atlanta looks back and says, "We haven't ridden anything." I assure her that I will bring her back another night and we will ride everything, but she isn't having it. She grabs my hand and drags me to the ticket booth. Once we get tickets, we go stand in line for none other, than The Extreme. My stomach feels nauseous just watching it sway back and forth. When it is our turn, I try to weasel my way out of it and she holds my hand and says, "It's okay… I got you." We take our seats. The ride slowly speeds up with every swing side to side. It lifts high off the ground, my eyes close tightly, and I develop a knot in my stomach. I am supposed to be the man, but I am deathly afraid of heights. Her hand sits on my leg and I squeeze mine tightly around the bars that are holding me in the seat. I won't let go, not even for her, because I know if I do, I will plummet to my death. Yes, I am a big baby. I admit it. I can drive one-hundred and eighty miles an hour with no problem, but put me somewhere high and I am going to scream like a girl.

Atlanta is waving her arms in the air, laughing and having the time of her life. She looks over at me and pokes her bottom lip out. Yeah right. She's not sorry in the least that I am terrified. I know inside she is laughing hysterically. I can't blame her I would be laughing at her if circumstances were reversed. The ride stops and we jump down off the seat. When my feet hit the ground, my legs feel like jello. I try to keep my composure so the crowd around me doesn't think I am a wimp-- a sissy boy, not capable of handling a small fair ride. Atlanta wraps her arms around mine and squeezes me into her. "It's okay, see. You made it. It wasn't that bad was it?" I give her the evil eye.

"Yeah it wasn't, that bad…" She laughs as we walk back to the car and drive to her place to finish what she started at the cotton candy booth.

9

Future & Beyond

Atlanta and I spend the next couple days interlaced in each other's daily chores and errands that we've put off since our newly found relationship status change. After buying groceries and going to the gym to workout we spend the remainder of the evening snuggling on the couch that has brought us so much joy. Game night has been a huge event in our lives since we both realized that we were competitive humans when it involved each other. Tonight's game is Rainbow Surge which consists of some serious Special Forces operations. We have only been playing the game for a couple weeks but it has become a favorite due to the bad ass uniforms and weapons. The way games are set up now it is almost like you are in the action that is transpiring on screen so we take this very seriously. Atlanta is so dang adorable when she gets in game mode that this is probably the best day of the week for me even over the street races.

"I got the game setup and ready. Do you want to wait for me to kill you before you eat, or would you like to eat first?" She questions from the living room.

I'm just a few steps away in the kitchen making us drinks in the new Kinky Girl tumblers that she purchased custom made for us that include our gamer names on them.

My gamer name is DareNdstroy while hers is GlitterAssault. Her name fits her perfect since more than half the stuff she owns has some type of sparkle to it. From glitter, to sequins and she usually does kick my butt at this particular game. Now if we were racing that would be a different story.

"Let's eat. I'm starved. Then I'll be ready for some Atlanta dessert." She giggles as the last few words slip out of my lips.

"I can see that we won't be playing until much later." She pouts poking her soft pink lips out before smirking.

I stroll over to where she is standing in the living room. "You know we will get to the point where you kick my butt in the game soon enough.

Let's go down to the Mouth Karaoke Bar and Grill and order a to go then come back here so you can kill me several times over before the night is up."

She agrees and we walk down to Mouth and order up two cheeseburger dinners with a side of fries and two strawberry cupcakes. Once we get back to the apartment and devour our dinner Atlanta proceeds to beat me at the first game of the night within the first twenty minutes. "Dang woman! Can't you just pretend you suck just once?" I joke.

"Now, what kind of woman would I be if I let a man win? You know y'all already beat us at a lot of stuff." She grinned a silly yet sweet smile. "You guys have to let us girls have our moments too."

"You are perfect at everything. I honestly can't think of one thing that you don't shine at." I plant a big sloppy kiss on her lips and she pulls away laughing while wiping the wetness off her face.

She leans in softly and before I realize what is going on she sticks her tongue out and licks my cheek. "Pay back!" She giggles.

I wipe my cheek and make a grossed out face. "Do you want to see what kind of game you have with some real guns?"

She looks at me puzzled. "Umm."

"I picked up two Nerf guns if you think you can handle it." I tease.

Atlanta puts on a serious face that is slowly breaking with a smile. "Handle it? Please, you are small darts compared to what I am about to hit you with."

"They are in the truck and I bought us a couple masks to wear. You interested in an outside shoot out?" I wrap my arms around her waist and pull her close to me on the couch.

"You know I am." She nuzzles my neck. Her head leans up and I press my lips to hers gently and hers respond instantly.

My whole life I have been longing for this life and now I have it. The sheer thought it would come true had grown to be a dream I ran out of a hope after all these years yet here we are, sitting on this couch about to go shoot each other with foam bullets in the dark. I couldn't have asked for a better life. Even if the car broke down and I lost my job, as long as I had her in my life there would be no regret, no sadness.

We climb down the stairs and wonder over to my car as I reach inside and pull out the plastic bag that is filled with masks and toy guns. I hand her a box with an orange rifle and a Jason mask. I slide the Freddy mask out for myself and begin opening the other box with a yellow gun in it. Each holds roughly ten foam shells that are attached on the side of the rifle. I load one in the chamber and she does the same.

"You go stand over behind the tree and I will stand by the stairs and we will turn our backs toward each other and count to five. Once we get to five we will turn around and begin to take aim. First one to hit the other, wins." I explain the directions.

"Be prepared to get dirty when your butt hits the ground." Atlanta chuckles as she runs over to the tree.

I'm actually a little scared after hearing that. I make my way to the stairs and turn my back toward her. "One…Two…Three…Four…Five." I jump facing her direction and get a glimpse of her dodging behind the car. I duck down and truck it closer to the car and just as she peaks her head out from behind the car I shoot, missing.

I fall to the ground and load the chamber all while looking for her out of the corner of my eye. She is small and fast so the only thing I have going for me is the white Jason mask standing out in this dark lighting.

I hear Atlanta's sweet voice.

"Put your hands up buddy." She makes a fake gun chocking sound. "Turn around slowly with your weapon up."

Damn. How did she manage to get so close without making a sound? She has to have some type of ninja gene in her blood. I turn toward her and hold the Nerf gun out. "You devil. You couldn't even fake losing." I whine as she shoots me in the chest. The foam bullet hits my chest and bounces off hitting the dirt. I grab my chest and fall backward leaning on the car. "Ohhh, my chest. You got me."

She strides over and leans into me hovering. "I told you I'd make you my bitch. Next time don't question my bad ass skills."

"Oh I wouldn't dare question anything you say. Without a doubt I know you own me." I grin.

"And with a smile like that I know for a fact that you own me too. Game over." She whispers before pressing her lips to mine.

Skid Marks

Saturday night finally gets here and I haven't felt this psyched since Atlanta confessed her feelings for me. She is wearing a simple black sundress with black strapped high heels. I can't help but stare at her in all the right places before focusing on her eyes. "You look beautiful." I tell her.

"Thanks but I already knew that." She smirks and twirls around. I smack her on the butt and she jumps. "Ouch. You know the material of this dress is too thin for all that."

I rub her in the same spot. "Sorry sugar. I'll be gentle next time."

We leave and head to the secret location only a select few trustworthy people know about. We can't risk the cops finding out so, in order to attend you have to prove yourself before getting in on the street races. Tonight's location is Old Natchez Trace Parkway Bridge that is just outside of Nashville, so Atlanta and I go down early and eat dinner at the Café.

She orders the daily special, which is a sweet and spicy chicken with green beans and hash brown casserole.

I can't decide from breakfast or dinner foods so I get the chicken and waffles. As we wait for our food to arrive, we look around at all the walls lined with signed photographs of famous people. We have been here several times before so we search for new ones we haven't seen before. She quickly finds one with Mr. Jones and even though she has seen it a dozen times before she still gets excited like it was her first.

We finish eating and walk around outside and stretch our legs before the big event. I have a golf ball sized knot in my stomach from the anticipation and I need to get the anxiety feelings out. This is the race I have always wanted to be a part of. One hundred percent pure street racing. No security, no easy track that is made for the cars.

The blue skies have darkened into a dark gray and the moon is full allowing enough light on the ground that you don't need a flashlight to see. Atlanta and I get in the car and drive a few miles further to the bridge. There are already a few cars down below on highway ninety-six in the parking lot looking up. They can't see the images but they can see the car lights passing which to some is good enough while others are pulled onto the side of the road. It is around one in the morning so there are barely any cars on the road, which makes this the perfect location for a run. I pull my car over and turn it around so it is facing the correct direction.

The number ten spot is a purple 1967 Plymouth Hurst Barracuda with a modified small block and five hundred horsepower under its hood.

The engine sounds are breathtaking on this beast and every time I have watched the owner race, his skills become sharper and he blows everyone away.

The owner is J.R. Buford and he stands at six-one without his cowboy boots and his muscular physic and long dark hair has all the ladies drooling while all the men look for the nearest exit. He is not like the others in this crowd. He comes from money and lots of it. As a matter of a fact, Atlanta dated him a few years back and I thought she would marry him but the jerk cheated on her with some bimbo from a club one night. Too bad for him. His sister told Atlanta's best friend Dani, and she told her. Now, here I am with his ex, trying to take his spot on the list. This can't go over too good.

Atlanta and I get out of the car and walk over to Wade who is preparing the other drivers for the race by handing out line-ups and informing them of the rules. I listen and pull Atlanta close beside me kissing her on her forehead. J.R. is watching us closely. He has always tried to get back in her good graces but she wouldn't have it. She deserves more and she knows it. I've always been a grease monkey with no means of giving her the fancy life J.R. can, but I will have her best interest at the front burner all the days of our life. I'll never forget how torn up she was when she found out who the other woman was. I got the call about two in the morning. It was pouring rain, but that didn't stop me from sloshing through the mud to get to her so I could try and piece back together what he broke.

After Wade finishes the run down on the nights festivities J.R. makes his great attempt of being the biggest jerk you've ever seen. He pushes through the crowd and stands front and center of Atlanta. He towers over us both and glares at each of us. "Is he why you won't return my calls?"

"Umm. No, you are the reason I won't return your calls. Remember the bimbo you cheated on me with? Well, that should be your first clue." Atlanta blurts out and tugs me away from him.

"Ignore him sugar. He isn't worth the H2O they are going to pour in his water box during his burnout." I lean in and kiss her.

She returns my kiss. "Tonight is your night. Don't let him ruin it. Take him down and I'll see you at the finish line."

She walks to the other end of the bridge with the rest of the crowd. I slip into the seat of my car and hit the furry white dice with black dots that Atlanta gave me yesterday as a good luck charm. It is such a small gesture yet it made a huge impact on me. Fighter pilots used to hang them above their instruments for good luck. She knows that my grandfather has a set of white fuzzy dice in his car and that he was a fighter pilot in the fifties. She always remembers the small details that make every event that more special.

I look to my left at J.R. and then back toward Wade holding the flashlight that will be like the red flag tonight. Once he turned the flashlight on, we both hit the gas pedal and start down the asphalt. The air is cool and crisp on my skin as we speed to the finish line-- to my love. I push the car to the limit and the engine roars under me.

The adrenaline in my veins rages and I push the car further. I take a deep breath and go to the end crossing the finish line without holding back.

The front bumper of the challenger coasts over the line just past my opponent's car winning the race. I slowly pull the car over on the side of the road, hit the brake, and slam the gear in park.

The small crowd runs up to the car hooting and hollering with excitement. I wave, open the door, and get out of the car and Atlanta wraps her arms around me jumping up and down. "That was awesome." She cheers and kisses me passionately.

Wade yells overhead, "Dare Andrews is officially in the number ten spot kicking J.R. off the list. Now let's move on to the next race between number eight and number seven. While the crowd moves back in place to watch the next race. J.R. drives his car off the road to make way for the following cars.

He doesn't get out of his car but sits in it watching us. My heart is racing when it all sinks in that I just won.

Relief washes over me and a little of the "in your face" attitude when I glance over at J.R sitting in his car pouting. *I beat you, and I have the woman.*

Once the last race is over and Lewis gets to keep his number two spot we walk over to Wade to tell him we are leaving. Just as we make it to where Wade is standing, we all hear a gut-wrenching sound of tires squealing. It is dark out but the moon light is just enough to see the large shadow coming toward us. My bodyguard instinct kicks in, and I shove Atlanta toward the opposite direction of the car coming towards us. Fast. The screeching skid marks are the last thing I hear before hitting the hard black asphalt and sliding across the road.

11

Lonely Room

My eyes gradually open with stinging liquid pouring down my face. A bright light glaring in them doesn't help the burn. I try to open them wider to see where I am and what is going on in the room but it takes a few minutes to adjust. Once they open, I observe a blonde nurse putting a clear liquid into an IV in my arm. "Wait." I manage to squeeze out of my frail voice. She takes notice and leans over me. "Sir, do you know where you are?"

I nod my head yes. "Atlanta?" I say praying she understands what I am trying to say but she ignores me.

"Sir, you are in the hospital and have some serious injuries but you are recovering nicely" She updates me.

"Atlanta? Where"? I force out again louder this time. She continues to ignore me more and I am beginning to get frustrated. I try to sit up and she pushes me back down with her thin arms. My strength is not enough against her force. She immediately calls for help. Several nurses come barging into the room which begins to spin. Why will no one just tell me where Atlanta is?

I see my parents come into my room. My mom gasps and places her hand on her mouth and my dad lays his hand on her shoulder. They both slowly walk over to the bed and the nurses' step back out of the way.

They appear to be so sad and distraught that I fear I may be dying. I want to see Atlanta's face before I go. I say her name again hoping that they will bring her to me but they don't. They stand still in the same spot staring at me as if I am about to pass on.

I can feel the pain in my stomach now and the pain is getting worse with every breath. I move my hand up off the bed and try to touch where the throbbing is coming from but my mom grabs my hand and clasps it forcefully.

"Son you and Atlanta were in an accident. Do you remember?" My mom mutters.

I shake my head no. I know I was in an accident, but Atlanta was pushed out of the way. Where is she?

"Atlanta is down on the next level of the hospital in ICU." My mom informs me.

"ICU! How? What do you mean? I have to get out of this bed and go see her. What happened?" Panic and fear rush over me. I rip the IV out of my arm and blood pours all over the cotton sheets and on the white tiled floor. One of the nurses wrap my arm in gauze while another one tries to restrain me to the bed. My mom and dad step back while the staff try to calm me down. I observe another one put something into my arm with a needle.

I struggle to keep my eyes open but they grow too heavy, and the medication takes over my body and I fall asleep.

I'm not sure how long I was asleep, but when I wake up it feels like days have past. My parents are in different clothes and the IV is back in my arm. I am strapped to the bed by what seems to be blue belts. This time when I try to talk, I can get my words out clearly and my dad comes and stands by my bed. My mom is already in the chair next to me and her hand is in mine, softly stroking it. She has tears in her eyes but I have to know what I can already feel. "Mom…dad, what happened to Atlanta?"

My dad glances at my mom and then back to me. "Atlanta was hit by a car. Some witnesses told us that you pushed her out of the way but it wasn't fast enough and the car still hit her. She is in a coma, Dare. We are told that it doesn't look good and we should pray."

My dad's eyes fill up with tears and my mom begins to sob. "I need to see her. Please take me to her." I beg.

Bruised Dice

I have an open wound in my stomach from where they had to remove some asphalt from my abdomen when I slid across the road. The nurse rolls the bed to the elevator and pushes the button for floor nine. Once it stops, the male nurse wheels me to her private room 1015. He pushes our beds as close together as he can without interfering with the mounds of cords and machines that surround her. She has a clear tube that goes down her throat and appears to be connected to a ventilator.

She has another tinier clear tube that appears to have some dark green fluid in it coming from her mouth and a yellow tube in her nose. There has to be fifty different medications connected to her IV line. There is an outsized lump in my throat and I can hardly breathe.

I examine her thin white frame and spot the scrapes and bruises from the accident. My heart skips a beat and tears fill my eyes. I thought I saved her. She was there at that bridge for me and I couldn't even save her. I reach down and caress her pale hand covered in tape to hold the needle in place. There are white restraints on her petite wrists and I can't help but wonder if she has attempted to move and that is why they have them in place. I observe her breaths and patiently wait for her fingers to move or her mouth to open.

There is no sign of life except the false hope of her chest rising and falling from the oxygen being pumped into her by a machine.

"Did they catch the person that did this?" I ask my parents who are on the other side of the bed.

"Yes, he is in an undisclosed location being treated for his injuries." My father responds.

"Who"? Is the only word I can muster out of my gritted teeth?

"They call him J.R. but I don't have a last name. He has a concussion and some head wounds from the impact." My mom updates.

The fury builds and I slam my hand against the wall closest to me. "Can I have some time alone please?" I glance up at them and at the nurse who is in the room monitoring us. The nurse says, "Please control your anger though or I will have to ask you to leave." I nod and they all step out. I take in a deep breath and begin to sob. Her hand is warm which gives me hope she is still in there fighting to come back to come back to me. According to the hospital board hanging on her wall, we have been here for three days. I scan the room for more indicators that will give me the information that I am seeking. When is she going to wake up? Will she wake up? What made J.R. drive toward us the way he did and why did this happen to her?

The anger festers deep below the surface and as hard as I am fighting the urge to scream or worse. I want to find J.R. and put him in a dark hole so he can suffer just as Atlanta has. I can't speculate on his reasons however, he was upset when he noticed Atlanta was dating me now and wasn't returning his calls. That must be his motive behind this horrific act. He had better hope she comes through this and the cuts heal or he will be have wounds that won't heal and a lost racing spot will be the least of his concern.

My tears continue to flow and I stutter out various lines that anyone in my place would say such as…please wake up, come back to me, and I need you here with me. She lies in the hospital bed tranquil and lifeless. I lay my head on the cold bedside railing and close my eyes. The salty tears have caused them to burn as the fluid builds up so the only thing left to do is shut them to get relief. I breathe in and out through the sobs trying desperately to bring some calm to my terrors. I feel a warm touch on my shoulder and it slowly trails down my back, rubbing back and forth. I turn to catch a peek at who has entered the room and my eyes open widely. I stare for a moment and then glance back at the bed beside me. Confusion rushes over me and I glance back at Atlanta standing beside me.

"How are you here but…?" I glance at the bed again. "There."

"Dare, I'm not going to make it. This is me telling you goodbye." She explains and reaches for my hand. "Follow me."

I grab ahold of her hand so tight that it would take a crowbar to pull us apart. We step outside the door and into the long white hallway. My parents are nowhere to be found and the staff is too busy attending to the other patients that they don't notice me leave. She leads me outside and to the centennial park across the street. The colors are striking fall colors, but the trees still have some green on them. We stroll along a path, still holding hands until we reach a bench just near the shore of the pond. We sit. She is so quiet for so long but I am in shock and I don't know if I am dreaming or if this is real.

"Dare, this is the end of the road for me. I have accepted it and now you need to accept it." She gazes over at me with a serene look on her face. I want to slap it off and make her fight to stay. To fight for me but I don't. I sit with one hand in my lap and the other one squeezing what life there is left out of her small hand.

"Damn it Atlanta! Why aren't you fighting?" I scream and release her hand.

"Dare, I fought hard and I lost. My organs are failing and my heart is barely holding on. Don't you think I have tried? I don't want to leave this world and I surely don't want to leave you. I love you Dare. You have been my heart for my whole life and only now were we going to build a life together and this happens." She unleashes the rage inside her but it doesn't make up for the fact that life is telling me this is it for her. For me.

"What can I do to fix you?" I look into her eyes. "Who do I go to in order to beg them for your life?"

"You can't beg for someone's life. This isn't a movie where God is standing by to change someone for the better. Don't you get it? You are already good enough. I was good enough. This is just what hand we're dealt but God did give me these moments with you. To help you cope with the loss and move on."

"I'll never cope with this." I throw my hands in the air, stand up from the bench, and walk over to the edge of the water.

"You never knew this but I wanted to get married here. Right over there by the flower garden. I was going to have my dad row me to shore in a small white boat and walk barefoot down the green grass into your arms. My dress was going to be exquisite with beading covering every inch of the sweetheart style top. It would be slim fitting until it reached the bottom and it would poof out into layers of beaded fabric and roses, leaving it with a Victoria era feel. It would have been beautiful." Atlanta walks over to me and wraps her arm around mine.

"Well then do it. Wake up and marry me." I demand as the tears stain my cheeks.

"Marriage is just a piece of paper and we had so much more than that. We have a lifetime of memories, a life together as best friends and then lovers. We never called each other a spouse but we were in every way that mattered. In our hearts we found our soul mates at a young age and we spent our lives with each other."

"It's not the same. I want more. I need more time with you. There aren't enough memories and I can't make them without you." I beg nearly dropping to the ground. "Please!"

"You have so much life still to live and I won't let you throw it away on false hope. I need you to make a life for yourself that doesn't include me. I'm gone now. I've made my peace with it. Dare, you are the love of my life and I know I am yours but there is room in that big heart of yours for someone else. Children, a wife. I've had a few days to make a list of pros and cons while you were in dreamland." She lays her head on my shoulder.

My heart aches. I don't want to hear any of the garbage she is feeding me. I hate whoever brainwashed her into believing that in the clouds is better than in my arms. She belongs with me here. No God deserves her the way I do. I've waited a lifetime for the few weeks we have shared. "Ugh, I hate this. I hate it more that you think this is best for you." I grunt and begin pacing and she follows me step for step.

13

Stairs

"I won't leave until you can accept this but I do have to go for now." She holds her hand out and points to the path we just strolled down earlier. It slowly moves up and turns into a stairway. It is unlike anything I have ever seen. "I'll never accept this." I inform her. The stairs get smaller and smaller as they disappear into the cotton candy like clouds. The road-like path is surrounded by fun colored pinwheels and peonies. A bright light streams down from the clouds and brightens the steps. I grab for her hand and she firmly clasps hers over mine. "I will return but I have something I must do. They are summoning for me." She turns and takes every step to the top and I watch her until I can't distinguish her anymore.

I stand there gaping at an empty flight of steps without hope of her returning. I won't budge from this spot. Especially, not if there is a chance she will return, and I'm not here to see her so can she disappear again. I think about her parents that are as worried and heartbroken as I am, and wonder if I should tell them so they can be here too, but I am too selfish to leave. Too selfish to let her go. I should be by her bedside waiting for her to wake up but instead I am here on this stairway path to nowhere waiting on her return. What? Why am I standing here waiting when I can follow her? The stairs are still here.

My feet step one foot in front of the other and I make it up the first few steps then glance behind me before proceeding up more. Once I get about ten steps in, I see something moving closer to me. It's her! "Dare, you can't come up here with me." She reaches me and pulls me to the bottom of the steps. She twirls backward and squeals. "Look what they gave me. Wings"!

"Wings are cool." I choke back the massive lump in my throat. "Can we just sit for a while and not talk about them or the wings?"

She takes a seat on the bottom step that appears to be made from asphalt, which certainly doesn't make me smile anymore. There was a time when the hard black road made me happy anytime I was on it, but now all I feel is agony when I see it or think of it. J.R. took everything from me that night at the race and all I took from him was a spot on a list. A list I don't care to ever honor again.

I turn to face her; my eyes are filled with burning liquid. "Why aren't you fighting for me?" The words barely leave my mouth when suddenly the phone rings. I ignore it, but they call again. I slip it from my pocket and look to see who it is, and a text appears on the bright-lit screen.

Mom: Come back to the hospital when you get this.

I glance over at Atlanta. "What's happening?"

"You should go be with your family. You can see me tomorrow. I'll be here when you get here." She utters.

I can't bear to leave this step without her, knowing that I am going to her lifeless body in that cold hospital room. I reach out and touch her warm face. "You feel alive to me. How is it that I can feel your heartbeat but you say that you are dead? Your smooth skin is so warm and your lips are moist."

"Dare, I am still me, just in a different place. You should see it there. I wish I could take you with me. It's like here, but with so much peace. Every day on Earth you struggle with judgement, self-worth, jealousy and more but in heaven everything is peaceful. You are surrounded by people that love you and there is no hate. You will love it years from now when you join me." She stands off the step. "I can tell you more soon, you better go now." She kisses me and begins her climb up the never-ending stairs.

14

Pain & Guilt

Back at the hospital room, she is still in a lifeless state. The doctors tell her parents and us that they don't believe she has any brain activity so they are going to run some tests. I personally think they are just blowing smoke up our ass, so we stop asking questions they can't answer. In the few hours I have been awake they haven't told me anything that has been fact except I have an open wound and a concussion that is more than likely causing my sudden ghost visits. Mr. & Mrs. Reed mention the doctors are talking about taking her off life support. How can they even think about that…after only a few days? I slam my hand on the concrete wall. I don't feel anything but I notice blood pouring down to the floor from where I gashed a knuckle. Tears flow down my cheek, but it's the thought of losing her that is killing me, not the pain from slamming my hand like a deranged psychopath.

Mrs. Reed brings me a washcloth and wraps it around my hand tightly. "We know, Dare. You aren't alone in this. We're so blessed to have you here with us. Just knowing she had someone love her as much as we did means everything." She stated as if Atlanta is gone already. "Do! I do love her and she isn't gone. She needs more time to heal." I shout before storming out to go to my own hospital room.

I need a break from those people already giving up on her, and I need to be alone. They have no sense of what fighting is. I've heard of miracles where the patient woke up years later from a coma. Atlanta can be a miracle damn it! If they turn off the oxygen then she will have to fight that much harder and she still needs rest. I need her to open her eyes when she is ready, not when they force her too. The ghost of her that I saw earlier today makes me fear that she has already given up on herself and ever coming back to me.

This hospital is louder in the evenings, then it is during the day. It seems that there is more being accomplished when patients are sleeping, then when they are actually awake. When I was in Atlanta's room I only saw one nurse the entire day I was in there.

I have seen four different nurses since I came back in my room. Each one had something new to do, and if they poke me one more time with a needle I am going to lose it. I'm not the one that needs help. I have been sewn up, while she is down on the level below me, not being mended.

In the early hours, the room is quiet and the halls are dark. I am alone. I want to pick up the phone, call her, and ask her to come play a game on the console with me. I want to touch her soft skin and smell the clean scent of her shampoo. Anything to have her near me. Something I spent every day of my life doing. If this is what the higher power has planned for our story, then I want to punch him in the face. I don't care who he is because he shouldn't be so cruel to have you love someone with your entire heart, and then rip him or her away without a second thought. I think about the stairs and how they are my way to her and then I feel guilty for blaming him for ripping her away when he gave me this.

I keep replaying the entire night over and over in my head. If winning wasn't so essential to me then J.R. would have won and maybe just maybe he would have left us alone. Maybe none of this would have ever transpired and we could have gone on with our blissful lives. If there was a way I could turn back the fast moving clock and change the way things materialized, I would. It's my fault, she was at the bridge that night, and it's my fault that she is lying helpless in that cold room. I wrap my arms around myself and slam them into my ribs. *Damnit Dare. This was all your fault.*

If I could have pushed her harder then maybe…just maybe, she would have been far enough away from the car that it wouldn't have hit her. I play it repetitive in my head. She consumed me; I wasn't watching the things that were happening around me, so I missed the car moving our way until it was too late. If I could have opened my eyes, I could have prevented this from being part of our story and she would be safe. I draw my legs close up to my chest and I begin to sob. In the dim unoccupied room, all I want to do is die. To avoid this pain and the guilt I feel, but for the most part to avoid losing her. I'm breathless and lost in a dark place with nothing trying to pull me into the light.

They discharge me the next afternoon and I spend the remainder of the day in Atlanta's room. I try anything to wake her up, from playing her favorite songs, to bringing up memories from our past.

The longer she lies there the worse I feel and the larger the lump grows in my throat. I feel like I am suffocating. I place my hand over my heart, my chest is hammering, and my heart is racing.

I'm helplessly immobile in the blue chair, my breathing is rampant, and I feel like I am dying.

A nurse rushes into the room and hands me a plastic bag to breathe in and out of slowly, "Sir, you are okay."

I relax and rest the bag on my lap. "Sir?" The blonde female nurse tries to get my attention. I look at her dead face. She repeats herself. I want to answer, but I don't want to live anymore, so I think if I ignore her then maybe she will go away and let me die in peace. Please just let me die.

"You are having a panic attack." She states.

Panic attack? Great, I can't die from that. Instead, I have become a basket case, a crazy person hovering in the corner of a white padded room, rocking my body back and forth. There is no escaping the overwhelming surge of the walls closing in around me, and no light at the end of the tunnel. The staff and both of our families are telling me she needs to be taken off the machine. Hell, she has told me I need to let go, but that isn't going to happen. I will stay here with her until they drag me away.

Everyone leaves me alone in the room again. Don't they know that when I am alone, I freak out the most? Every single time I sob until I can't breathe, or I just stop breathing all together. I don't like it, but then again their negative vibes aren't helping Atlanta fight either. Its best they stay away and don't let her hear the rubbish they keep spewing all over this room. It's only been a few days since the accident and they are already writing her off.

Dr. Anderson has convinced her family there is no reason to keep her on the ventilator anymore and from what I have observed, they are just waiting for the okay. They don't check her blood or barely come into the room anymore except to change some medications from time to time. Those bastards.

I stroke her soft hair as I watch the machine expand her lungs with air and then release it. The noise from the ventilator is odd but it gives me hope that it is working. Hope is all I have left.

15

Anger & Bargaining

Days pass, and I have only left the cold room to use the restroom and get some food. I can smell myself from not showering. Mrs. Reed found out from the staff that there is a shower I can use down the hall in the doctors' lounge. I am pretty sure they are tired of my stench. I take the bag of clothes my mom brought me a couple days ago, and enter the bathroom of the lounge. It's nothing fancy like I imagine for a doctors' lounge. The same basic hospital bathroom with a toilet, sink and shower. There are white tiles that cover the entire floor and go up half the wall. The shower reminds me of something you would see at a campground site.

I adjust the water to my liking, undress, and step in. I have to admit it feels good on my skin and I almost feel alive again. I lather up and scrub my body from top to bottom. Once I am finished, I stand under the hot water until it begins to get cold.

I step out and dry off. Above the sink is a large mirror. I stand and glance in it. It's been nearly a week since we have been here, and it shows on my face. I look dead. My eyes are dark and sunken in, and my skin is pale probably from lack of sleep or food. I can't go on like this. The weariness has weighed on me like an anchor holding a boat steady at sea. I need answers.

Unless I have lost my mind, then I need to visit the stairs that she said she would be waiting at. I get dressed and throw the towel in the blue hamper next to the door once I am finished.

I make my way across the street and down the path to the clear lake area that I was at days ago. There is nothing there along the path. I knew I was a flipping crazy person. I sit down on the ground, and stare off at nothing. I close my eyes, take a deep breath, and get up off the ground. Then I notice that the stairs have formed. A warm sensation washes over me. I don't know if this is my brain playing jokes on me, or if this was real, but I decide to treat it as if they are real and I begin to climb to the top. Once I am several steps in something comes over me. I start to yell. I can't take this crap anymore.

"Hey, I want to talk to the ruler up there. Send him to me!" Nothing happens so I continue to climb and with every step, I scream louder, "Bring her back to me.

Please, I beg you. If you won't, then take me too before I take myself." I am angry. The rush of adrenaline has turned me into a beast, and not even the all mighty creator could defeat me. I yell some more.

Legs. Legs for days appear in front of me, strolling down the stairs. Her voice is strong. "Stop! You need to go back down. You're not allowed up here. My heart feels like a ton of bricks are crushing it from the inside out.

I start walking backward because my eyes are fixated on her. I am terrified if I stop for even a second she will disappear. "Why are you screaming like a mad man"? She glares at me. We reach the bottom step, and I sit putting my hands over my face. "I'm pissed off okay. That jerk took you from me. I'm mad that you have given up." I remove my hands and shift my head to glare at her.

My body is shaking from anger, and my jaw tightens with the built up tension.

"Don't you think this is hard for me too? To see you with my parents by my bedside, crying, and not eating. It kills me, but this is it. There isn't a do over in life. Once you're gone, you are gone. You have to embrace what you had, and move on." She grabs my hands in hers, kissing them gently. Her hands are warm sending chills down my spine.

"I'm not ready for this. Please fight. Do it for me. Beg the ones upstairs to let you come home. Your body is still here and the machines are keeping you alive. There is a chance they will cave." I plead with her, squeezing her soft hands in mine, not wanting to break the connection, and not wanting to lose her warmth.

"Don't you think I've already done that? His reason is simple. I had my life with you and now he has chosen me to be there with him. I'm an angel." She tilts her head back toward her new white wings. They sparkle and are larger than I remember. "You were already my angel." I let go of her hands and stand up regretting the loss of connection the moment my hands are free. "I lived my whole life for you. Waiting for you to see what was right here and you can't even, not die for me." I growl and storm off walking down to the edge of the lake and kick the green grass along the bank. Guilt rushes over me after my outburst.

"It's not up to me. I'm going to stay here as long as you need me. It's simple, really. Soul mates are not taken from each other forever. In the end, they will be together. It might not be in this life, but it will be in eternity." Her smile is soft. My heart melts whenever she is around, dead, or not. I notice the glow surrounding her body. This must be what an Aura looks like. It's so stunning like her own personal stage lights.

It glows every inch of her frame with just a small touch of light. It's not noticeable to most people. You would really have to look at her, and know her soul to catch a glimpse of this beauty.

"I don't want to spend the rest of my life waiting for the day I can climb those stairs and join you." I gaze in her eyes and readjust my legs while the sadness of it squeezes my heart, and takes my breath away.

"You need to live. Fall in love with someone else. Have children. You're going to have to let go of this…of me." A small tear pours down her cheek.

It's about time she is showing the emotion I have been unsure was there anymore. I figured the afterlife wiped away all those hard, down to the core feelings and left her with happiness. It doesn't make me sad for her that she is crying but elated that she still has a soul in there at all. After days of her willingness to leave and join the angel cult, it feels good to know a part of her will miss the human life as well. There won't be a wedding day for her, children or a life with me and those things shouldn't be easy to brush aside for a pair of wings. I don't care how peaceful it is where she is going; you don't just forget the things you have always dreamed of before your departure from Earth.

Breathless

It's been two weeks since the horrible accident that put Atlanta in a coma. The physicians have done all they can do, and today is the day her parents have decided to take her off the ventilator. The trees have started to change color from green to golden yellows and oranges for fall. This is Atlanta's favorite time of year. She would rake the brown leaves in her tiny yard into a big pile, and jump in them over again until she is too worn out to rake them up one more time. She grew in height and in life, but she always remained a childlike soul throughout adulthood. She always kept me on my toes and taught me to not take life too seriously. Now here we are about to end the miracle we have prayed for every second since the accident-- since the assault on her.

Mr. And Mrs. Reed and I gather around her hospital bed. Our friend Dani, my parents, and a few other friends and family members are outside in the waiting room. We are all going to say our goodbyes before they turn the machines off and then her parents and I will sit with her quietly and watch her take her last breath.

Fans are outside the hospital which has turned into a media circus, but the candles and prayers do bring some much needed love to the place. I'm not ready for what I am about to feel and I am not ready for my future.

Some people say life is more painful than death and that it should ease our grief knowing our loved ones have moved on to a better place. I've never seen the other side. Heck, I've never even heard of anyone going there until I was on that park bench and the stairs appeared before me. I do find comfort in knowing they are there for me, but what about everyone else. I make a mental note to ask her about that when I see her again. For now, I will hold on tight to our friends and family.

Dani goes into Atlanta's room alone. We all give her the privacy she needs, and we sit in the waiting room for her to return. My parents sit next to me and rub my back like they did the first time I missed the winning catch for my little league championship. I felt as if my whole world was over then. Little did I know I would be facing an even greater pain years later?

If I would have known, I would have told myself to do things a different way. It's too late to go back now, but I will forever hold the guilt for the rest of my life.

Don't wait for the right time in life to get what you want. Pursue what you love now, and live a lifetime without regrets. I can't second-guess everything in my life up until this point, but let's face it, now that's all I have left. In a few hours, she will take her last breath, and leave this earth for what she calls the perfect world. She was, hell, she is my perfect world.

Dani comes out red faced with blood shot eyes and tear stained cheeks. I rush over to her and wrap my arms around her small frame. I can't fight back the water that has been hidden behind my eyes while everyone says their goodbyes. The floodgates open and there isn't any going back. My body heaves and my arms tighten around her. "I can't believe this is our life now." Dani whispers and grips the back of my shirt in her hands.

I hold on to her for what seems like a lifetime, but reality hits once I hear the sobbing, no…It is screaming from Atlanta's mom down the hall. I squeeze Dani's hand once more before letting go and make my way to Mrs. Reed.

When I reach the room, I stop at the gray hospital door that is open wide. Mrs. Reed is kneeling on the ground with her hands covering both sides of her face. She lets out the most painful sob I have ever heard, and Mr. Reed is at a loss as what to do to help her get through this tragic event that involves their only child. "Help her." A soft voice echoes in the room. I turn and see Atlanta glowing beside me wings and all. My breath stopped or maybe it had already stopped the moment I saw her in this hospital bed, but she is breathtaking. The tattoos that covered her body are rich in color and the purple highlights in her hair are deep and compliment the natural chestnut brown. Her blue eyes have always been a crystal blue, but now they are like the blue lake in Colorado that you have to hike for hours to get to. Mesmerizing.

"What can I do?" I murmur trying not to disturb her parents.

"Let them know I am okay. Tell them I am happy where I am and safe," her blue eyes begging me to protect them from all this pain. Pain that I am feeling too. Pain that is unbearable in every way. I would rather be stabbed a thousand times in the eyes then to ever feel this way. She wants me to help heal them when I am crumbling. Atlanta wasn't a ninety year old with a lifetime of memories behind her. She wasn't sick for years and this takes away her suffering. No, damn it! She was in her twenties and had a quarter of memories to take with her, and she was healthy and talented. She had so much to offer the world…to offer me.

I take in a deep breath and pad my way over to Mrs. Reed. I know she can't feel her legs to stand, so I sit on the cold nasty hospital floor next to her and wrap my arm around her. Her arm flies up and she grasps my shirt with her hand. Her breathing is erratic and as hard as it is I manage to hold back the tears and the emotions and do what Atlanta asks. "Atlanta loves you and knows how much you love her. She always told me how blessed she was to have you both as parents and that you gave her the best life. Though, we might not feel it now, someday we will understand why this happened and why we are left here to figure it out while she climbs a flight of stairs to Heaven and sings with Angels." My words must have moved her, or maybe her legs have had too much, but she stands and I help balance her. Mr. Reed lays his hand on my shoulder, takes his wife's hand, and leads her out of the room.

I gaze over to the corner, and Atlanta is still standing there looking as if someone switched on her inner light. "I guess I have to say goodbye." I utter the words, but I don't mean it. I'll never tell her goodbye. "Will you still be at the stairs when this is done?" My voice shakes as I say it scared of what she will say, but I ask anyway.

"Until I know you are ready." She assures me.

I have so many questions, and she is here for me to ask but let's get real for a minute. I'm talking to a ghost and now I'm asking her when she is going to leave me. I should ask when I get to leave here and be with her. I know she will ramble on about how I have so much more life to live. I'd like to shake some sense into her or anyone else that says that crap. I have to let them think they are telling me what I want to hear. It's not that I want to die, instead it's like I already did.

As humans, we are taught death is something that happens when it's our time and if it's not, then we have to live without the ones we love. Don't we stop living once we lose them? I question myself.

"I'm not telling you now. It's not the time and I'm not ready." I lean down toward the bed, kiss her on her forehead, and brush her hair back with my fingertips. Your body might be gone, but your soul remains here with me. I refuse to give that up and let you go. If you're not going to fight then I'm going to need the stairs to see you until it's my time to go." I lift my head up and glance at Atlanta. I'm not sure if I should call her a ghost or figure of my imagination but it's enough for me either way.

Hours have passed since the machine was turned off. The nurses remove one bag of medication after another followed by the machines and monitors until the room is nearly empty. Her parents stand at one side of her bed and I at the other. The doctor stopped in a few minutes ago and told us it would be any moment now. When the time came, we held her hand and didn't take our eyes off her. Her mom whispered to her one last time that she loved her and her dad assured her it was okay to let go. I didn't say a word. I wasn't giving her the satisfaction to have my okay to leave me. I'll never forget her last breath for as long as I live. It was frightening, heartbreaking and left me breathless.

17

Depression & Loneliness

I left the hospital and went to Atlanta's place. The story had broken that she had passed away and her fans surrounded the building with candles, while blaring her music across the street. Beside the stairs to her apartment, there were teddy bears, handmade posters, and flowers piled all the way to the entrance. I stopped for a second and then for one moment I smiled. Not a happy she's dead smile, but a smile from the knowledge that she was loved by so many. She had only begun the journey to stardom, but she had built a huge fan base over that short time. Her music helped them through the hard times and the best times in their lives. I turned and nodded in the direction of all the people that were outside paying their respects.

I turned back and went into her cold and empty place. The smell of incense surround my lungs as I shut the door behind me laying my keys on the table like I always do. It's been a few weeks since I have been here. Nothing has changed. I don't think Mr. and Mrs. Reed have stepped foot in here since the accident. For me this is where I spent most of my time other than work so I want to be near her things, smells, and in the place we became one.

I grab a beer out of the fridge then open the closet door and climb down to the second floor. I walk over to the country section of vinyl and find one of the sappiest songs my mind can muster and place it on the turntable.

I lift the needle bar up and lower it onto the spinning black record. The mellow voice of a male artist and the lyrics fill the room. I sit against the wall and pull my knees up to my chest. The warm tears roll uncontrollably from the corners of my eyes and down onto my lap.

I feel an empty void in my chest where there once was the largest amount of love. Now, it is hollow like a pumpkin that has been carved out and everything that makes it whole is removed. All I feel is barren. Tears cascade out of my eyes from the empty cavity. I pull out another record that is her. Atlanta's first and only gold record. I remove the old record and place hers on top of the turntable. After I sit the needle on it, I kneel down on the sag carpet beneath my feet and I sob. Her voice feels the room and I picture her face, her crystal blue eyes and I wish she was with me. Just like the first time we sat and listened to it together. She was always her biggest critic and I her biggest fan.

I return upstairs, shower and then I curl up on Atlanta's side of the bed and bury my head into her pillow. I take in a deep breath and inhale her scent. I feel a soft hand on my back and I know its Atlanta. I roll over to see her lying in bed with me. "I'll never get over you. There isn't anything that will cure this disease I now have." I stroke her arm lightly with my fingertips.

"There is always one thing that will help heal your pain and that is time." Her face peaceful.

"There isn't enough time for an antidote." I spit back. My voice is angry and hard.

"Dare, you need to start focusing on the good in all this. Now you know there is a heaven and you know I'm okay. At least this way you aren't left wondering like so many others about their loved ones after they pass," her words flow out of her pouty lips, but all I hear is I'm dead.

"Dead. You are dead. Maybe this isn't for me but more for you. Maybe this is a way for you to cope with the fact that you are no longer living." The anger builds the more I talk but I'm pissed off. It feels good to be mad and lash out at her. She needs to see how this is affecting me. I want to pull her back to earth. I want to punch the face of the God that took her from me. You can't sugar coat death. It is what it is, and it's pure crap. There was no reason for her life to be taken, but there is many reasons to give her back. Marriage, kids, grandkids. A life.

I roll over and close my eyes. I can't look at her. She doesn't smell like herself anymore. Her skin is softer than I remember and the glow surrounding her takes away from the simple beauty I remember. I want my Atlanta back. I want her the way I remember and not the way she has now become. My mind plays tricks on me however I am no longer fooled by her presence. She is a ghost. A figment of my imagination.

I fall asleep. I don't try to feel her around me and I don't hold on to the fact that I can see her. I am too angry to let her win. If I give in and accept that she is gone, then the ghost will leave and I will be left here alone.

My dreams are full of her. She sits on a wooden bar stool with a guitar in her lap, strumming the strings and humming. I love the melody filling the room. It's the song she wrote for me.

It's not recorded which angers me more. I'll never hear it again. My heart crumbles into a million pieces. More loss. More reasons.

Morning comes faster than I wanted. I am not ready to face the day again so I close my eyes, and drift off again. My eyes burn from no moisture. The tear ducts are tired and have shut off while the pain in my head builds from the pressure. My phone buzzes on the bedside table. I open my eyes, lift it up, and see that it's my mom. She's worried.

Mom: Dare, we want to know you are okay. Please answer us.

Me: I'm fine. I'm at Atlanta's apartment. I just need to be alone.

Mom: The funeral is tomorrow. We will come pick you up at eleven.

Me: Okay

A freakin funeral. I have to bury the love of my life and my best friend all in one day. She is all I've ever needed and poof just like that, she is gone. I pull the covers over my head, roll over, and close my eyes. Atlanta says she's okay with being dead, so if I lay here long enough maybe I can die too. It surely has to be better than the pain I am feeling right now. The huge lump in my throat and the massive pain I feel in my stomach. Yeah, death would be better than this.

My phone buzzes again. I slam back the blankets and pick up the phone. It's Camry. *What the hell!*

Camry: I heard about Atlanta. I am here if you need anything.

Me: Thanks

I push down on the power button towards the top of my phone and slide it to off. I need to be alone. I am alone. No amount of people on this planet could make me feel different. She was my world and now there is nothing left.

I slide my head back under the comforter, and fall back asleep. There is no one I want to talk to and no one I want to see.

The next thing I know, my mom is shaking me. "Wake up, son."

I growl. "Just let me sleep, ma."

"Archer Dare Andrews. Get up now. If you don't go today you will regret it for the rest of your life."

"I already regret going." I murmur back.

"Boy, don't you talk to your mama like that. I know today is hard and you have a lot to deal with but now is not the time for self-pity." She rips the covers off my body.

I stumble out of the bed, stomp my way to the bathroom, and shut the door. My mom yells through the door. "Ten minutes."

18
Casket & Me

I ride with my parents to the church. Why her parents insisted on this church, I'll never understand. Atlanta wasn't the type to sit in a pew and listen to a preacher. She would more likely turn on a church program on the TV before dressing up and heading to the building itself. Sure, she believed in God and all, but she lived her life the way she thought was right and that included the tattoos. Once, she went to this same church with her parents and overheard from the ladies talking about how God didn't agree with the markings on her body. She never returned to that church or any church after the way they made her feel.

She used to explain to me that it was her way of expressing how much she loved something. I never quite understood how inking her porcelain skin made her feel, but I always accepted it. Her skin was like artwork. Every color and every image had a meaning. My favorite one was the words; I only move the stars for me. It is written in elegant cursive on her collarbone. It's small but somehow it makes the biggest statement even compared to the sleeve of intricate designs.

My dad parks the car and we all get out. I notice fans and news crews covering the block. Atlanta was just starting out on the road to stardom but she had already made her mark.

People were holding purple balloons in the shape of a heart all down the road. I took in a deep breath and proceeded to walk behind my parents. Dani runs over and grabs my hand. I want so bad to pull it away but I can't move. My knees feel weak, and my heart is racing. Dani is our closest friend and she is hurting as much as I am. It wouldn't be right of me to push her away and Atlanta would kick my butt if I tried too. Dead or alive- she takes care of the ones she loves.

The preacher shakes our hands as we walk inside the large cold sanctuary. The walls are white with light wood trim. The high ceiling spans the entire length of the room with a massive chandelier in the center. Flowers surround the room and directly in the center near the pulpit is a casket. It is open, but I can't bear to get close to it.

I freeze in my spot and take in everything around me. Atlanta's parents are up front near the casket, hugging and greeting people as they come close to them. How can they stay so calm with their daughter lying there lifeless?

I take a step over and take a seat in the pew next to me. My parents continue on their way up to the Reed's. They love Atlanta like they love me so I know they are hurting too. I just can't understand how it is so easy for them to hold themselves together, and to go up there and look at her face. I'm afraid I'll climb in it and close the lid. I'm more afraid that I won't be able to leave her side, so I'll just sit here and try not to make a scene.

A slide show of her life plays above us on a large screen. Images of her childhood through the current year stream for all to see. I glance around and see all the people that are here. I've been to everything Atlanta has ever been too and I don't notice half of the people here.

I know she touched lives and I know she was loved, but where were all these people on the days she was fighting to accomplish her dream or had a flat tire? Nowhere. People think just because you are related or that you know the person's names then you are entitled to come to their funeral and share the one time you had an encounter with them. Shouldn't a funeral be where the ones you are closest to get to say goodbye without having to fight over who gets a turn to gawk over the lifeless body in the casket?

Some people stop by me, and pat me on the back or hug me. I don't give them a chance to start a conversation. The last thing I need is pity from the fake friends that only are here to get a glimpse of the dead girl so they can post some sob story on social media about how they were here and how sad it is. Dang right it's sad. It's sad to those who really care. The fans that are die-hard or the family members that were at every birthday party, to the friends that I can count on one hand that bought every song on their music device.

Atlanta's songs play in the background. The one that touches me most is the one she sang at Mouth Bar and Grill in Palm Coast Florida for the first time with a young girl named Callie. It was the first time she sang a song that was written by someone else, and I'll never forget the fans reaction when they heard it. They were in love with her and her voice moved them. That was the beginning of newfound success for her. Her true calling in life was to make people feel; not just your average feelings, but also the deep down in your gut, sway to the beat, and experience every moment of the song kind of feelings. Moments like that you don't just remember, but you relive every time you think about it.

The service was short yet overwhelming. The preacher talked about God, and how life has just begun for her and a lot of other garbage that is supposed to make us feel better. It never makes anyone feel better. Most of us are whispering under our voice to shut the hell up. I know that in these moments there is nothing anyone can say to help the pain, and everyone tries to come up with something but they really should just shut the hell up. We know they care yet their lame attempt at meaningless words mean nothing when your soul has been ripped out from under you. We just need hugs and a shoulder; beyond on that we aren't listening.

The room empties as everyone lines the road with their cars to drive to the cemetery. I am left alone inside with only a casket. The flowers have been taken to the site and now the funeral directors are waiting for me to leave.

Now is my chance. See her one last time or leave and only talk to the ghost in my head. I'm not sure if my legs can make it to the casket but I figure it's now or never.

I stand and I lift one leg at a time and place it in front of the other, continuing this process until I am only a few steps away from the wooden box. I can't see inside but the outside is light brown oak wood with purple lining. The flowers on the lower half of the wood are purple and white peonies with sprinkles of baby breath and greenery. She would have picked this out if given the option. The large cold room is silent which makes the hard thumbing of my heartbeat annoying. I let in a slight breath, and release it in the cool air, repeating in hope that I will pull myself together.

My foot trembles when I try dragging it closer to the box. It is so weak, I almost lose my balance and fall face first into the casket. My heart beats faster with every step. I close my eyes before I reach it.

I can feel the lump in my throat move down into my chest. The wretched pain clouds the sadness just in time for me to face her. My lifeless love. I pry my eye lids open, and look down into the silky light purple area.

Atlanta lies there still and just as stunning as she was living. Her face is a little bloated and slightly more pale than when she was alive and breathing but it looks like her. Beautiful. Her mom picked out the perfect outfit for her to wear. Atlanta wore this on her first day of touring. A simple white sundress with lace trim and boy, did it have the twirling factor. She would twirl around and sway back and forth to each of the songs she sang on that stage in Atlanta Georgia. She wanted it to be the first stop on her tour since her name and life were both given existence in the city.

I am unable to control my urge to touch her so I reach inside and stroke her hand. It is cold as ice and stiff as a log, and I don't know whether to continue or to let go and forget the feeling of her motionless body. I want to go back to the warm-blooded body that held me as we made love, and those sweet lips that kissed me goodnight. Instead, I am standing here clasping a hand that feels like a frozen banana. I wrench my hand back and bring it to my chest. Staring into the casket at her tranquil face, I let the emotions rush over me. "Atlanta, my entire life has been to love you. Now that we are in this place, I don't know how to move forward without you. I don't want this to be the end of our story. We were supposed to have an eternity together and now you are telling me it is over and my entire future existence is a waste. I love you. I will love you to the stairs and back." I turn on my heels and stroll down the aisle, feeling empty and purposeless as I make it out the door to my parent's car that is already in line for the ride to the cemetery.

19

Liquid Gold

It has been a week since the funeral, and the only things I have done are eat and sleep. The last thing I want to do is get up and go through the motions of living, when drowning by my own saliva sounds more appealing. It is the start of a new week and I have to go to work. Edward has given me time to grieve, but now I have to work so I can pay the bills. I haven't driven the challenger since the accident, and I am thinking about selling it all together. It feels like a curse. I knew getting everything I ever wanted was too good to be true and it was. Atlanta's car is in her driveway next to my truck and I can't help but picture her behind the seat when I walk to mine. I feel a heavy weight in my chest whenever I see it.

If that car could talk, it would tell you all the mind-blowing memories we had in it like the time Atlanta peed on herself from laughing at a joke I told her. I'll never forget her reaction after she realized what she had done. We were driving home after beating two men during a highway race in their 2014 Mustang cobra. I dramatized the joke as much as I could about a blonde girl that was on her computer and it kept telling her she had mail so she would get up and go out and check her mailbox. Seeing that it was empty, she was confused as to why the computer would tell her that.

As dumb as the joke was Atlanta couldn't stop laughing and unfortunately, for her she just drank a big gulp. Her bladder couldn't handle the pressure from the laughter and it released. She made me pull over at a small pond and the stripped down into her bra and panties and ran into the cold water. After splashing around and washing off her soiled panties, she ran out and threw her shirt onto the seat and her pants into the floorboard of the car. We drove to her house while she only had the pale pink wet delicate on that clung to her body. We had the heater cranked up on high and I was sweating buckets, but it was still a memory I won't forget. I loved observing the way she turned an embarrassing moment into something enjoyable and worth remembering.

I made it to work ten minutes early so I proceeded into the break room and made a cup of coffee in the stainless steel mug Atlanta bought me. I can't help but think of her while I dispense the steamy black liquid into the cold metal, then it occurs to me that every day I am going to be exposed to things that will bring up her memory.

It's hard enough to breathe without her near me, much less having to get through moments that remind me of her. I don't know how I can do this for the next fifty or so years. I hear that it gets easier with time yet; I don't want anything to be easy. I want it to be hard, that way I will never forget what we had. Forgetting what we had would mean it didn't exist, and it most definitely did.

I stroll out to the garage and start working on a 1951 Ford F1 pickup. The original factory motor was taken down and rebuilt to perfection involving the rear end, brakes, and front end. The outside color is candy apple red with black cherry fenders and matching running boards.

Once the interior is finished, it will be candy apple red with black leather seats. The grill is a shiny white that will tie it all together. Edward leans on the doorframe, "How's it going?" Men don't get gushy with other men so I nod and simply say. "It's going." He understands, and wanders back into the office.

I have to admit working has made the day more bearable to get through. I clock out, but continue working for a couple more hours. The time flies by and the day turns to night. I clean up around the shop and lock up behind me on my way out. I climb in my truck and sit for what seems like hours yet is around a total of five minutes. I begin to drive to Atlanta's place but something changes my mind. Instead, I pull into a small dive bar called Dancing Bottles. I feel like tonight I should drown my sorrows with a bottle, or more of the cooling liquid that comes in a clear bottle from behind the bar. The bar is set up similar to an old western one. It is covered wall to floor in cedar wood, the bar is a standard long bar with leather side rails.

Behind it on the wall is a mirror that stretches from top to bottom with shelves full of liquor. I bark, 'Wild turkey' at the bartender and he nods. He is in his fifties with salt and pepper hair that plays peek-a-boo under his tan cowboy hat.

He slams the shot glass in front of me, and pulls the bottle of WT off the shelf pouring it into the glass before gliding it closer to me. "Leave the bottle." I state before slinging the liquid gold down my throat in one gulp.

"Take it easy. This stuff will get you in trouble." He pours the shot again when I sit the small glass down in front of me.

"Trouble is what I'm looking for." I hiss.

The bartender walks away and waits on another customer. The voice seems familiar so I twist my head and gaze in that direction. It's Camry. What the heck is she doing in a rundown place like this? *That girl sure isn't your typical rich girl.* I turn back away so she doesn't notice me. The last thing I want is to be bothered while I am trying to drink away my blues. I sling back another shot and fill the glass again while the burn rushes down to the pit of my stomach. This is going to be one heck of a hangover tomorrow but I don't have a care in the world.

A few shots later I am beginning to feel the buzz and it is a little tricky to keep my frame on the bar stool. I slide one leg down on the hard wood floor to help balance myself. Last time I drank this much Atlanta and I were celebrating the end of her first tour and we had a big party at my place. It was an old fashioned bonfire and she had at least a hundred people there congratulating her. The morning after people were still partying and some even passed out on my lawn. It was wild but unforgettable.

"Dare. Is that you over there?" Camry raises her voice from across the bar. She hops off the stool and walks toward me.

Great. That's the last thing I want tonight. "Yep." I don't want to be rude but it's just not the right time for me.

"I don't come here ever, but I was looking for some quiet time and when I passed by I thought this would be the perfect place to get away from the Nashville scene." She informs as she takes a swig of her longneck bottle.

I nod. "My thoughts exactly." I drink another shot. "How's your dad?"

"He is such a fighter. My aunt Lisa is over at the house now so I can have some free time. She watches after him so I can get out of the house from time to time." Camry tucks her blonde hair behind her ear, and a memory of Atlanta flashes in my drunken mind.

It wasn't because she looked anything like her, but because when Atlanta would tuck her hair a small black star tattoo that was just behind her ear peeked through. It was the first tattoo she got after she signed with Smash Records and I loved it. Atlanta loved that her skin was a work of art and tried to get me to cave and get some tattoos, but I never knew what I would get that I would want branded on me for the rest of my life. She loved things so much that it was easy for her while I just loved her and it would have been creepy to have her tattooed on my body.

"Do you plan on drinking your night away or are you doing something more interesting?" Camry asks as she slides her empty beer out of her way and waits for the bartender to bring her another one.

"I was planning on drowning in the bottle tonight, but now I think I am going to a tattoo parlor." I throw some bills on the bar and stand up. I tilt my head down to her and tug on my old White Sox baseball cap. "I'll see you around. Say hi to your dad for me."

"Wait! Can I go? I've always wanted to watch someone get one of those things." Her big eyes beam at me.

"Suit yourself. I need a sober driver anyway." I hand her my truck keys. "Have you ever driven a truck?"

She grasps my hand and gives me the keys back. "No but we can take my car."

I slide my keys in my front pocket and follow behind to her car. What is it with this family and classics? I stop cold and balance my feet. None other than a 1969 Chevrolet Camero blue with white race stripes down the middle. I scratch the back of my neck. "Did your dad build this?"

"No he purchased this one for me when I graduated high school. He said he had one just like it when he was a teenager but it wasn't nearly as pimped out." She runs her fingertips down the hood before opening the driver door. "Get in."

I open the slick passenger door and slide into the white leather bucket seats. "Who does your custom work? I've never seen you or your dad at Ed's until that first day."

"My dad did everything with the challenger himself and ordered parts online from various stores. When I got the car, it was already refurbished except I added the air conditioner. It's too hot in Tennessee to be without it." She puts the shift handle in reverse, and backs out of the parking space, shifts it to drive she drives downtown.

20

The Love that Remains

She pulls into a mid-sized parking lot, parks the car and turns the car ignition off. We both open the door in unison and step out, shutting our doors. "So, do you have a parlor in mind or are you going to go to the first one you see?" She questions before walking in any direction.

"I am going to see Atlanta's favorite guy. Harlem Lottham at Stained Ink. He knows me from the countless times I have sat in the corner and watched her add to her body.

Camry follows close at my side as we walk the couple of blocks it takes to get to the tattoo parlor. I guess a girl like her has no life after taking care of her ill father for so long. That has to be the only thing that would explain her wanting to come watch me be branded by needles. I feel sad for her and the life she has endured. A mom that left her behind, and a father that had no choice but to check out of life. Fortunately, she has her aunt and possibly more family that can hold her hand through the pain.

We reach the parlor that sits in between two swanky bars that were never Atlanta and my scene, however I think Camry would actually prefer them over the dive I ran into her at earlier. The inside of the parlor was remodeled a little over a year ago and went from drab to downright bad ass.

The floor is concrete that is painted to look like marble and the room is surrounded by large floor to ceiling windows. Half the room is painted a deep red while the other half is a slate gray. My favorite part of the room is the back wall that is sporadic, covered in dark wood planks. It is like a work of art in itself. The waiting area is donned with simple black leather chairs, a plain black coffee table, and a large silver drum that is used as a side table or perhaps it is there to add to the room.

Atlanta started coming here when they first opened five years ago. Harlem did her first tattoo. I'll never forget how scared she was at that moment. I sat there as she squeezed my hand nearly off. At one point, I thought she was going to pass out because she turned a pale blue shade. The tiny music notes made her giddy when she saw it on her shoulder in the hand held mirror that, Harlem held up when he was finished. She was hooked.

The saying is that once you get one tattoo you can't stop and she proved that to be true. After, a full sleeve and several others later she took a break at adding them saying her canvas was complete. If she were here now I know she would take that back and get one with me.

Camry takes a seat in the waiting area in one of the leather chairs while I go up to the counter. Harlem sees me and nods. The cute brunette with a short bob greets me. "Hi Darc." Her words purr, "Is Atlanta joining you?" My heart skips a beat. "No, umm… It's just me today." I don't know what I was thinking coming here. Coming to this place with all these memories and they not knowing. Wait, how does she not know? Atlanta's death was all over the news. Harlem strolls over and pulls the young girl to the side. He must have informed her because she glanced up at me and excused herself to go outside. A look of pity drenched across her face before walking out the front door.

"Hey man! Sorry to hear about Atlanta. I hope that jerk gets what he deserves for what he did."

"He will." I murmur biting my lip hard so I don't go off the deep end. "I want to get a tattoo."

"After all these years you have finally decided to brand yourself permanently. Cool. What are you thinking?"

"I want a hawk with the word *Saudade* around it. Do you think you can come up with something tonight?" I ask. If I wait, I might change my mind and I am tired of pussying out.

"Yeah man. Let me finish this client and I'll sketch something up." He shakes my hand and heads back to the man sitting in the dentist type chair in his section. Harlem doesn't own the place but you would think so since he is so popular here.

He told us years ago the owner doesn't even have a tattoo but wanted to open a business that wouldn't be hard to run yet would make him some money.

I take a seat across from Camry, and lean back in the cold chair.

"What's with the tattoo choice?" She questions.

I lean on my knees and rub my forehead in a circular motion. "Hawks are messengers of the sky and observers. I thought it would be perfect since that's where Atlanta is now, and the word well…it means, the love that remains. Every moment we shared will always remain here with me." I point to my chest.

Her eyes fill up with tears. "That's beautiful Dare. I…I am so sorry this has happened to you….To her."

I stand up not wanting to talk about it anymore. "Thanks." I whisper before I pad over to the window and stare out at all the people strolling by without a care in the world. Almost all of them will take the ones they love for granted and waste life on meaningless material things. No one lives to be happy anymore. It's all about money and fame. What ever happened to being as happy as a kid on Christmas? The feeling of excitement waking up that morning knowing there is something magical in the day. We should live to have that feeling instead of living to be rich with green paper. The invisible riches end up outweighing the ones you can see. Love is what living is about. True undying love.

Harlem holds up the sketch once he is finished, and the image is powerful. He knows Atlanta well, and he knows my love for her. The image features a hawk with wings spread wide down the length of my arm, a colorful pinwheel is center in the one eye shown then a thin white ribbon wraps around the body of the hawk with the word, *Saudade* perfectly written in a script font. I manage to catch my breath after seeing a piece of art, which has Atlanta written all over it, and murmur, "Let's do this."

Angel wings & Me

Camry dropped me off at Atlanta's apartment a few nights ago, and that's the last I have heard from her. I still never found out why she was alone in that run down bar, but I have turned into a selfish guy with one thing on my mind and it isn't naughty like most men. I should try to be the person I've always been but I won't. I have no desire to go through life lying to the people around me about my feelings. The truth is, I am angry and the only thing that helps me get through the pointless days is knowing I can see her.

After work, I meet Atlanta down at the foot of the steps. I go so frequent now, I don't have to call her and wait for her appearance. She is ready for me once I start strolling down the path to her. The snow-white feathered wings span the entire width of the staircase, but she carries them well. She is always stroking them down by her side as if they are some sort of pet. The more we see each other the more I am jealous of her new life…or maybe it's called her afterlife now.

She seems to be in this place of happiness all the time and never complains about not being able to see her family or do all the things we did while she was still here. I'm jealous that she can be content without me.

I spend my days working and nights filled with empty drinks to soothe the pain.

"What would you like to do today?" She leans in and kisses my cheek.

"Do you think we can go to the record store and listen to the oldies like we used too?"

"The one upstairs won't allow it me to leave this area anymore. It's okay though, we can listen to music in your truck since its close." She reaches for my hand and of course, I take it.

I open the door and allow her to slide in and I follow suit. Her wings fill the cab of my pickup leaving me enough room to sit. For those passing by I'm sure they think I am crazier than an ex-girlfriend on crack by the way I am sitting crunched up on the driver side door. I turn the key in the ignition halfway so the radio begins. Conway plays in the background as she lays her head on my shoulder and we sit in silence. It's different being with her now. I try and pretend it's the same but she doesn't feel the same. She's softer, warmer. No matter how long we sit here, it will never be enough, and it will never bring her back. I always thought she would come back to me, but the more time passes the more I am getting to know this is all I will ever have. It used to be Atlanta and me against the world, and now it's me against her wings.

"It's not the shag carpet in the record room, but I have a blanket behind the seat." I go to pull it from behind the seat and she giggles. That sound. I've missed her laughter more than anything through this all. Pain fills me. Gut wrenching pain severing through my flesh.

"I have a perfect external temperature now, but it's sweet of you to think of it. You were always the gentleman. You are going to make some woman a lucky lady someday. Just, Well… I hope it's not Camry." She glances up and I notice her eyes rolling.

"Jealous even in the afterlife huh?" I can't help but be amused. I run my fingertips down her wings. "It will always be you I want. Not even death can change how I've felt my whole life. My existence was meant to love you. I can't picture a world without you, and in all my twenty-three years of life I don't see me with anyone else. I never did."

Her eyes show some sign of caring. They build with tears and while she doesn't want to let it go, at least now I can see something authentic. All this talk about how the great afterlife is perfect for her and now I see it's not exactly true. *She misses me.* I needed to feel as if I meant something too. I ache nonstop and it wasn't for nothing, it was for her. I can convene here all day, but when the time comes, and I have to crawl into my bed all alone, it would be nice to take with me that she did love me.

That no matter how jealous I am of her new life, that there is still a part of her that would want to be with me if she had a choice. That I mattered.

I don't know if I can go on living the way things are. Heck, I don't even know if I can wake up tomorrow and go to work, but I know she loves me. I did see it in her eyes for a moment. It might have been a brief minute but I feel it now and even with my heart-breaking, knowing that helps. It doesn't take away the pain but it soothes it.

One oldie song after another plays on the radio as Atlanta and I sit in silence. We don't have a future to discuss anymore, and she can't tell me about what happens up those stairs. Let's face it, there isn't one anymore. I don't want there to be one without her, so I will work until the time passes and I grow old…or if I'm lucky I can get struck by lightning and it lead me to the staircase to heaven. I can't picture myself walking around with massive wings on, but when the time comes I hope they are manlier than the frilly ones Atlanta has attached to her back.

"Tell me about the wings. Are they glued on, or are they like boob implants?" I break the silence. Atlanta leans her beautiful face up to me and beams.

"They are like implants I suppose. I got to choose the ones I wanted too and they come in different shapes and sizes." She strokes the feathers.

"No dark ones huh? All white and fluffy?"

"How many angels have you seen with dark wings?" She glares at me before bursting out in laughter. "Just kidding, Dare. You can have green wings if you want. Apparently, a few years back things changed and the big guy changed his view on the way things in the clouds were handled. Angel wings now can be in a rainbow of colors. He said there is no distinction between men therefore, we should be who we are and not who we are told to be. It's beautiful up there. I chose white because it looks BA next to my tats. Don't you think?"

"Yes they do, sugar. I was about to run the opposite direction when I saw you because I was so startled." I poke fun at her. Her tattoos have dark elements such as the skulls, but on her they are stunning.

She lifts up my sleeve. "I saw you do this and it's lovely. You know I am always watching over you. Even with flights of stairs between us, there isn't a second that I am not thinking of you, or watching to see what you are doing without me."

"I'm full of entertainment huh?" My heart sinks with pain wishing she was by my side instead of watching me.

She kisses my inked skin softly near my tattoo but not on it. "You could give me something more to talk to my friends about."

"I'm not sure if I am ready for that just yet, but I'll see what I can do."

"Why aren't you driving the car?" She asks the hardest of all questions.

"I just don't want too." I push up on the seat to sit up straight.

"Why Dare?" She questions again, her tone firm.

"It reminds me of your death okay. I don't need anything else in my life to remind me that you are dead. When you are upstairs in the rainbow winged clouds having a great time and watching me suffer down here it isn't because I am sad, it's because I am dead too." I exclaim throwing my head into the back of the headrest, the tears trailing down my face.

"Atlanta, you just don't understand what life is like for me. I sat day after day watching you leave me. You didn't even try to come back to me; you quit, walked up those stairs, and didn't look back."

She shifts her body toward me and abruptly screams a loud screeching scream. "Damn it Dare, I'm here. I did look back. I saw your heartbreak and I came back down the stairs for you. I can't give up my wings because it was my time to go, but I am with you until I know you are okay without me."

"Just know that there will never be a day that I will be okay without you. Not one damn day!" Fear overtakes me at the thought of her not being there at all. My body begins to shake. "Atlanta." I lower my voice, "Not one day."

22
Foolish Nights

It has been a one month since Atlanta departed this life. The days aren't easier, and I work until Ed makes me go home. The evenings I consume enough alcohol to numb the agony until the next morning. I visit Atlanta every evening before I drive myself to the closest bar and indulge in anything and everything that is tossed my way. Women surround me every night and try to get me to take them home and some have even tried lacing my drinks with something so I will cave. The women always ask how I am and give me their meaningless sympathy about Atlanta's, but that is what it is…meaningless.

Atlanta never scolds me or brings up the fact that I have turned into a total lush, but I know she sees me. We spend our evenings listening to music as we did when she was here in the flesh and not a ghost. I don't turn the radio on when I am alone. There is no more music played at the garage while we work, instead Marty wears a headset when he isn't rambling on about the night before. It's nice to hear him talk without bringing her into the conversation and he makes it a point to avoid her or any music at all costs.

Even though the nights are the worst, I manage to make it home to Atlanta's apartment and my new home in one piece. I put my house up for sale and moved all my stuff into the record store.

Damon likes having me around since I take care of any other repairperson work he has, and can no longer keep up with. I have a free upstairs apartment and he gets all his grunt work done without complaint, except what he doesn't hear from me, like how the smell of the incense reminds me of her, or that every time I climb into the closet to go down to the second floor I turn around to help her down, and she isn't there.

Tonight after I fix the downstairs bathroom door that keeps jamming on Damon's customers I decide to go to Dancing Bottles and let loose. I have already had a couple drinks when I feel a soft hand caress my shoulder, Hello, handsome."

I take in a big gasp of air and annoyed I turn around to see what bimbo it is. To my amazement I lock eyes with Camry. I feel my heart speed up a little. "Hey stranger. Where have you been these last few weeks?"

"My dad passed away so I have been coping and getting all of his things situated for an estate auction happening this weekend. You should come." She takes the bar stool next to mine, crossing her long legs.

I get a whiff of her amazing smell when she saunters by me. "I'm sorry to hear about your dad. I wish you would have called me so I could have been at the services. I only met him less than a handful of times, but we were connected through metal and rubber. The man knew cars and that I admire."

"Thanks." She chokes up. "He wanted a small service which only meant my aunt, her husband and myself. He said that people were going to stare at him for years until he passed, therefore he wouldn't allow anyone to stare at him once he did. He was right.

People can be so rude when it comes to someone that is different. Someone not their idea of normal."

"I completely understand. For years I watched people gawk at Atlanta with her tattoos trailing down her arm, and at her colorful hair. She didn't have a disease, but I would always catch people staring as if she was a creature out of the black lagoon. Different is beautiful in my eyes, mentally and physically. Atlanta's beauty was not only on the outside, but deep within her soul.

Once, while she was on tour she noticed a young woman in a wheelchair in the upper level. During a costume change she had one of the crew members bring her to the side of the stage with her family. I'll never forget the girl's face, and how her brown eyes lit up as Atlanta sang. Moments like those aren't for the extra media attention, but instead are sincere and from the heart.

"Have you decided what you are going to do now that you won't be taking care of your dad?" I nod for the bartender to bring me another beer.

"No, not really. I knew this was going to come one day, but I never dreamed it would be so soon. You know, even the most expected death can leave you in shock. I always knew the moment was coming, but I thought it would be years from now." She lays her chin on the palm of her hand being held up by her small tan arm.

"When Atlanta died I lost myself. Hell, I didn't think I would be able to survive another day and here I am one month later still going through the motions.

It's quite possible I will never move past the shock. It's as if I am still standing in that hospital room watching and waiting for her to wake up.

There is part of me that wishes I could follow her where she went, but the other part is scared to find out that they won't let me in and I'll have to go through eternity without her." I take in a swig of beer. The ice cold liquid numbs the itch that is building in the back of my throat.

Camry's face softens. "Dare, what would you say to her if you had a chance?"

"Well to start with, I would tell her leaving was a huge mistake. That we could have had a lifetime of memories instead of half of them. You know what I've already told her everything and she doesn't listen. She left and now she haunts me." I peer down into the hole of the longneck bottle. "We were soulmates. She was mine and she left me like I wasn't hers."

"You know it wasn't her that chose to leave. That was out of her hands. Just as my dad left me without a choice. We will never understand the reason why people die however I think their spirit always remains with the ones they love. I talk to my dad like he is here. Maybe you should do the same with Atlanta." Her hand brushes against mine.

I turn and gaze at her. "I have. It doesn't change anything. She's still gone and I'm still stuck here on this earth living a life that is already over."

Camry reaches out and clasps her hand into mine. "Let's go."

She doesn't need to say anything else. Atlanta made it clear that she didn't like Camry, and now I can make her feel some of the pain I have felt for the last month.

The sun streams through the sheer white drapes. My eyes burn as I open them. Camry's scent fills the air as I take in my first morning breath. The night before me is foggy, and I try to make sense of where I am and why I am here. I growl. Why does alcohol make people so stupid? Atlanta might be in Heaven, but when she marches down the stairs later today it will be like she is in the flesh. I can't lie to myself, I'm looking forward to it.

23

The Upward Turn

Atlanta was so angry when I saw her last night at the stairs. I still can't believe how mad a ghost can be without speaking in an angry tone. She was sort of devilish, yet sweet at the same time. I've been haunted by her words all day at work. "If she's what you want then you should be with her."

It's like she wants me to be happy, however she hasn't liked Camry since she first met her. Some female vibe she had with some mixed in jealousy. I can see now with the situation that is the front burner of my life, and her afterlife, how being jealous would fit in. However, even with Atlanta off in another world, unknown to me, she is still the only one I want.

Camry was a mistake that was plagued by booze and emptiness. I feel bad for Camry. I sense she has other plans for our friendship, and all I did was make it worse. Dragging her along my complicated life without one care for her feelings is quite rude, but in my defense, I never wanted it to happen.

Ed walks into the break room and opens the fridge, pulling a can of Mountain Dew out. "How are you doin? I try to stay away from the emotional talks in the garage, but I'm worried about you."

"I'm okay."

Popping the top on the can, he takes a sip before sitting at the table across from me. "Okay means you are going through hell. I've been there, kid. When I lost my brother a few years back. I can remember just how "okay" I was. You can't hold it in. You need to grieve and you need to stop drinking the pain away."

Ed has always been a smart and observant man and in more ways than I can count, he has read between the lines when it comes to my feelings. A few years back he told me to suck up the fear and tell Atlanta how I felt. I didn't listen since I'm stubborn as a mull, and it has crossed my mind several times that I have wasted from fear of losing her.

"I know. To be honest, I don't feel like living, but I know I have too. For her and for myself. She wouldn't have wanted me to be alone and if the tables were turned, I'm sure she would move on." I take a bite of the roast beef sandwich I packed.

"Here's the thing, Dare. We aren't put on this earth to have everything our hearts desire. That happens only when we go off to the place us humans call heaven. That's when we live happily ever after. Life isn't about fairy godmothers and magic wands, but instead it is about living the best life we can until we can reach the doors of heaven. Only then, will we be granted everything we ever desired." Ed takes another sip of his soda.

His words stick in my head like sticker to paper, and over the next few days I make a resolution. To let Atlanta go. As hard as my life has been without her body here in the flesh, and how much pain I will have to endure not having her body around in the ghost form, the time is now.

If I continue down this path, I will never say goodbye, and I will be stuck in this same place forever. I tried keeping myself busy so I wouldn't recognize she is dead, but a person can only be busy for so long before their world comes in focus. There comes a time when we have to stop and look around at our life and notice something huge is missing. A whole person. A best friend and love of your life.

I finish up my day and leave work when the garage closes. Tonight I head home to Atlanta's place and spend the night looking through her photo albums and listening to vinyl on the small portable blue turntable she kept on her dresser. The sad music fills the room and I sit cross legged on the bed turning one page after another. The memories flood my brain and the tears fill my face. I talk to her as if she is sitting next to me, but I know she isn't here with me anymore and my decision weighs on me. The staircase is a figure of my imagination in order to keep her here with me. The reality is…I've lost her and no amount of stairs will take me to her.

I close up the albums and place them back in the box before sliding it under her bed. I stand and pad into to the bathroom and turn on the shower. The water is blistering hot, but I want to feel the sting. I need to feel it in order to get past the emptiness in my heart. I am going to close the door to this chapter in my life tonight, but before I do I am going to say goodbye.

I find myself standing in front of the stairs within the next hour, and as I am waiting for my love to join me I begin to feel like a hollowed out pumpkin. I'm missing the part of me that fills my shell and it is not only the best part of me, but it is irreplaceable.

The angel shines before me. Her long brown hair blows gently in the wind. It's like a scene from a movie with her as the leading role. Atlanta has embraced her new glorious afterlife, and it looks spectacular on her. I can only hope I can take in my new life now that she is gone. There were weeks that had passed and I wanted to rip my heart out for the hopes of connecting with her, yet I stopped myself before acting on my sadness.

Death is unexplainable to us humans because we don't see what comes next. There is no proof that another life exists after our souls are taken from our body and our eyes close forever. There is no hope left for the humans that await their journey up the stairs. The only thing we are left with is pain, emptiness, the what if's, and why didn't I say this to them while they were here.

Now as I stand here with the love of my life and my best friend, it isn't what I always dreamed it would be like. I would imagine the most beautiful day and she would be glowing, wearing white, standing next to me and I would say the vows that have been etched into my heart since the day I fell in love.

"Atlanta, I have loved you since the day I saw your sweet smile as you took my transformer, and tried to put a frilly dress on it. I have been with you through the ups and downs that life threw at you, and I grew to love you more when I experienced the things you never wanted anyone to see. Like the way you drool while you sleep. Today, I promise to love you for all eternity and I promise to let you go free so you can explore your new life beyond the staircase. Today, I will let you go, but one day I will take you back, and when I do…I'll never leave your side again."

24

Acceptance

Today marks the first day my body is able to move without me having to force it to. The energy that has left my body before has decided to make an appearance and it feels great. I didn't realize how much I let myself go until I decided it was time to live. My muscles ache from lack of movement and my face and skin seem as though they have aged ten years during the last few months.

A few short months that have felt like years. People expected me to just pick myself up, and move on past the pain without a thought or mention of her, as if she didn't exist. I never quite understood how some men or women could find a new spouse or lover within the first year of their loss. It happens, but how do you let go enough to open the doors for someone else?

I walk down the block to a small quant café to meet Dani. We haven't spoken in a few weeks, so after listening to the twentieth message on my voicemail, I decided it was time to join the real world again, and that included one of the other humans on this planet that Atlanta loved as much as me.

I walk in and notice her sitting at the far back table near the restroom. I stroll back to the small wooden table, and pull out a chair that is covered in red and white checkered fabric, then I have a seat.

Dani's hair is now a dark blonde with a bright purple streak peeking through the fine hairs that are tucked behind her ear. I look away for a moment. It's a sentiment of her love for her best friend, and as hard as I've tried to move on, that gut wrenching feeling deep inside me is always lurking behind the wall waiting to take over again. As easy as it would be to fall apart and let it consume me, I know I can't go down that path again. The pain is too massive. I wouldn't survive.

"You should stop by the gallery. I have the photos for you put away." Dani breaks the eerie silence and the lump in her throat makes the tone off pitch.

I look down at the menu that lays flat in front of me. I've eaten here so many times with Atlanta and Dani that I could recite the entire thing from front to back and again back to front. "I'll stop by this week after work. I am almost finished refurbishing a 1978 mustang and once it's done I plan on taking a day off. The shop has been slammed with new arrivals. Ed is one happy feller with all the new clients. It helps to keep me busy and my mind off the things that could destroy me. How are you holding up?" I pause and slide the menu to the side of the table to alert the server we are ready to order.

"Not good. I can't hold back the tears. This morning I was walking down the block by my gallery and I glanced up and observed this woman carrying a small child and I began sobbing. I feel pain that I never knew existed." Her eyes glisten from the moisture that is breaking through, screaming to run down her sweet face. "She will never experience her own children."

"You know J.R's parents got him a fancy lawyer from Knoxville that is supposed to try and get him off by pleading insanity. His alcohol level was over the legal limit and they found drugs in his car." I close my eyes and take in a deep breath. "If they let that bastard go free, I don't know if I can control my anger."

The server pads over to our table and exclaims, "The usual." She looks at Dani and then me. She already knows the answer, but she still asks to be polite. We nod and the short haired blonde turns on her heels back to the register to put in our orders. The last time we were here, Atlanta ordered an extra meal for the homeless man at the corner. She had a soft spot for the ones less fortunate but this one man in particular made her heart bloom with emotion. I believe it was because he wasn't a beggar like the others but instead he sat on the corner playing a harmonica. Sometimes he would play songs that you knew while others were made up. He told Atlanta once that he used to chase after his dream of playing in a blues band and that's what lead him here to Nashville. His perseverance is what she loved and one reason why she never gave up on her dream. When the waitress returns with our drinks, I place a to-go order for the man in honor of Atlanta. I know she is looking down on me and smiling.

"When is the next race?" Dani questions with a slight stutter.

"I'm not sure. I've stepped back from that crowd since…since the accident. I don't know if I'll ever go back."

"It's none of my business but you have to try to enjoy the things that Atlanta and you did together. You know once she told me that seeing the sparkle in your eyes when you were behind the wheel of a fast car was better than the feeling she got when she was on stage. She said seeing you so happy brought her more joy than anything else in the world."

My heart sinks inside my chest cavity. "I'll think about it."

Once lunch is over I walk Dani to the curb and wait for the cab to come pick her up. We hug for a short moment and I promise that I will stop by and get the artwork this week. As hard as the pieces are going to be to look at every day, I can't help but remember the moment Atlanta and I first laid eyes on them in the gallery. Each canvas and sculpture represent our life as friends and as soulmates. Dani made her first sale off of those, but she printed copies for us yet Atlanta never got around to see them in her house. The only things I won't have are the hands.

The lucky bidder will have those for their self. I never got to meet the proud owner since Atlanta and I split early due to unseen desires, but it's pretty awesome that they could see the magic between the couple in the pieces. Once Dani leaves, I walk the meal over to the man on the curb. He is extremely grateful.

Homeless man: "Where is your lady friend?"

Me: In the shortest version I could mutter out I explained, "She recently got into an accident and didn't make it." My heartbeat nearly stopped when I saw his saddened reaction.

Homeless man: "So sad. She was the only person that never looked at me with pity in their eyes." He placed his hand on my shoulder. "Son, the good ones never really leave the earth. Instead they follow their loved ones closely and watch over them."

Me: "What's your name sir?"

Homeless Man: "Vince."

Me: "Vince, it's nice to meet you. Atlanta is looking at us now and I know she is smiling. Thank you." I extend my hand out and clasp it in his.

Vince: "Oh no sir, thank you and your lady for the meals and respect." He nods and sits down pulling the to-go container out of the plastic bag.

I take a short drive just out of town to my house. I haven't been there in a couple weeks but I wanted to pick up something close to my heart. Soulmate is just another word to some, but I learned to write her name before I did my own and I wrote it every day after in a journal that my grandpa gave me. It was a small leather bound book, with an elastic band to hold it together. After the first few years of writing in it every day the small papers soon became so thin from reading them over and over that I had to start a new book, and pack the first one in a box so I wouldn't cause any more damage. It's the one thing I never showed Atlanta for fear she would think I was less of a man because I kept a diary.

She never showed me much interest romantically so the last thing I needed was for her to think I had a limp-wrist. Not that there is anything wrong with that but I wanted and needed her to see me as the man of her dreams instead of her best friend.

I decided it was time to pull out the journals and let her read them. Dead or alive its better late than never. I stacked the four leather books back into an old boot box that I took from under my bed a couple hours ago so I could reminisce about her. I slid the box under my arm and locked the house door behind me just before getting into my old pickup and driving to the one place I knew she would be waiting.

I park the truck, grabbing the worn box and carry it to the small bench that sits near the huge never ending staircase and I wait. In only a few moments the winged goddess makes her way from the clouds and to my feet. She is still just as radiant as the last time I saw her. "Please have a seat. I want to show you some things that I have for you to read. The things I remember about our life. I want you to see why there will never be another love for me."

Her face is calm and she nods in agreement. Her wings retract just enough that she can sit next to me on the bench. I open the box, I pull out the first brown book, unwrap the rubber band and turn to page one.

"Marry Atlanta."

I continue to read through the small sentences that a young boy my age at the time could write. I close the first book, and continue on to book two. I have made it to the fourth grade and things begin to get serious.

"Today she told me she had a boyfriend. That little punk Jarred from Mrs. Mellon's class. I can't believe she thinks he is good enough to hold her hand. Her sweet hands are only meant for me."

The pages turn, and every day I have written how I continue to wish it was me that was on the receiving end of her kiss, the one holding her hand and saying I love you. I stop at a worn out page that is coming apart from the middle seam and I begin to read.

"The eighth grade end of the year dance. I will never forget this day for as long as I live. Atlanta didn't want to take a date so she instead, asked me to go with her so the boys would leave her alone. She was going through some independent stage where she wanted to prove her worth without a boyfriend or some crap. Whatever the reasoning, I was so over joyed that we hung out for the entire evening. Brushing off one boy after another. We danced all night to the popular club songs and the slow ones, and boy…did we slow dance. The closeness wasn't like the usual every day touch that I've always had with her, but it was like feeling the warmth on your skin after a long period of time outdoors in the snow. The butterflies in my stomach were beating the inside black and blue as I held onto her and spun her around the concrete gym floor. Not only do I know without a doubt, that I love her, but I knew in this moment someday she will love me too."

Her beautiful angel face shimmers in the evening moon light. "I hate that I took so long to wake up and see what has always been in front of me. I hate it even more that you spend every day living what is left of your life still loving me. I'm dead. I'm in another part of the universe that you can't enter unless you are dead. Dare…I don't want this life for you, yet. It's not time for you to join me.

Instead, it is time for you to live out the rest of your days enjoying the moments that are yet to come. Falling in love again, marriage, babies."

She pulls in a soft sob from beneath her words. "I love you to Pluto and back, but it's time for you to move on away from these stairs and toward a new life."

"Don't you see, that's what I'm trying to do? I want you to see that I've loved you a lifetime. I will love you for eternity, but until the time comes that I get the pleasure of walking those stairs with you, I will live. I will always live loving you, and no amount of time or circumstance will change the way I've always felt. It's in these journals I've written since I could only write short sentences, and it is in my heart where you have always been the beat of my heart. You are my heartbeat." I close the leather pages and place the journals back into the shoebox. My heart deeply aches and even though I know I have to move on, I also know my heart will always settle back in to the one thing it's always known; I love her and only her.

25

Gated

I closed the gate that evening. I said my final goodbye to Atlanta on that wooden bench. I haven't as much as driven by the park that lead me to the stairs or to her, but I think of her with every breath I take. It's been four months since that moment, and as I look around the apartment and glance at each stunning image that hangs of us on the wall from Dani's collection, I feel Atlanta around me. We didn't have enough time to be lovers, but we had a lifetime to be soulmates.

Tonight, I get behind the wheel of the car that changed my life for the worse. I am not dumb enough to think it was the car that killed Atlanta. I'm smart enough to know that JR's drugged rage was the reason for my loss, but it's taken me until this point to see that. JR was sentenced for manslaughter in her death and won't be eligible for release until he is in his seventy's. The anger is still there, yet I can't let it consume me anymore. Atlanta was right; I need to move on.

I park a couple blocks down from the strip and walk the remainder of the way to the Mouth bar and grill. Camry has been taking me to every bar in town and tonight is no exception. I'm not turning into a lush or whore, but I find comfort in the music, and this bar in particular brings me the most. She is a sweet girl that deep down I think has good intentions.

"Hey, Cam. I am meeting Dani in a little." I inform as I pull the bar stool out for her to sit.

Camry sits a bottle of beer in front of me on the bar. "Okay, that's cool. What's your week been like?" She pauses and I give a polite smile, grab the cold glass in my hands and press it up to my lips, taking in a long swig. "We are working on a new truck. A classic Ford. You should stop in and see it when it's done." The words flowed out of my mouth before I even had time to think about them. It seemed so natural to have her around.

"I'm taking a spin around the track tonight in the challenger. You can come watch? Dani will be there." As I say it I am reminded that I noticed Dani and Camry have been spending a lot of time together lately. Heck, they've become good friends. I could never figure out how they knew each other outside of that one day at the race track, but they seem to have a lot in common. Dani needs someone in her life that she can spend time with and do all the girl things that I don't want to do. Dani needs someone in her life that doesn't remind her of the best friend she is missing so I don't question it.

Her face lights up, "I'd love too. Can I ride with you? My car is in the parking garage down on the other side of town and I took a cab here."

"Sure, we will pick Dani up at her gallery."

I finish the beer and nonchalantly reach out and grab her hand. She doesn't pull away from me, but instead she smiles bright and follows close behind me, clutching my hand tightly.

We stroll the few blocks to my car and once we reach it I open the passenger side door for her, and close it behind her once she is in. It feels like any other night that I would be going with Atlanta, except it's not her. Being with Camry is a great distraction from the things I want to forget, and since she is interested in cars we have things to talk about.

She taps the dice hanging from the rear view mirror and they begin to swing. "Nice touch."

I grab them so they stop moving and reply coldly, "Thanks."

It's not that I don't want her touching them, or that I mind them swinging. Heck, they do that when the car moves, however it's that I don't want her hands on something only Atlanta has touched. That's the last gift she had given me and I cherish them more than anything else.

I am distant for a moment which seems to be my go to mood for at least half my day. Camry must notice and changes the subject. "The car still runs great." She exclaims, tapping her hand on the dashboard.

I come back to earth. "Yeah, this is the first time I've driven it since." I stop mid-sentence and try to find the words, but there is only one way to describe that day. "Since the accident." I decide to go with accident when all I want to say is murder. J.R. didn't accidentally hit her, he plummeted over her as if she was asphalt. My face begins to heat as the anger fills me.

"Let's talk about anything other than this car or the accident." I say through gritted teeth.

"Okay." Her word is soft. "Dani has become a good friend. I'm glad I'll get to see her tonight."

"When did you two start talking? I thought you only knew each other at the track that one time." I question.

"I stopped by her gallery and bought some work from her a while back. She has a lot of talent." She looks out the window.

"Yeah. Atlanta and I have been pushing her for years to open the gallery, and when she did it we were stoked. I know she will go far with that."

We pull to the curb right outside the gallery, and I excuse myself to go inside and let Dani know we are here. On the way inside I can't help but to smile when I see the window scene with a photo of Atlanta on stage with beams of stage lights covering every inch of her small frame. No one would notice it was her, but I, for one will never forget that night. After her huge set, she called Dani and me onstage to sing an old country song with her. We were totally toasted and the words slurred out, but Atlanta being the only sober one at the time helped pull it off. She was my country singer hero, right down to her cowboy boots. We spent the remainder of the evening trying to get Atlanta trashed, but she insisted on being the designated driver. It's a good thing too, because Dani nor I could walk a straight line much less drive.

I have it on video somewhere. A fan sent it to her that evening. Like the box of journals, I have a lot of pictures and videos I should go through when I have time.

Dani might like to have some for her collection. I have a feeling she has her own stash lying around somewhere.

I open the door and pad inside and notice Dani walking from the back. She slings her tasseled purse over her shoulder and yells, "It's about time you showed up here. I've been closed for thirty minutes. What held you up? A hot lady?"

"Well, actually yes. Camry is in the car. She wanted to ride with us over to the track. She was in Mouth and the words just slipped out." I smile a crooked apologetic smile.

"I'm sure they did." She chuckles.

"I have to throw her a bone sometimes. She stalks me like a tiger trying to catch his prey. I feel sorry for her and its harmful." I nudge my arm into hers.

"I'm riding shotgun and your stalker can zoom in her camera lenses from the back." She laughs louder than before, locking the front door behind us. I look back at her and shake my head.

26
Empty Staircase

It feels strange pulling into the track. I don't feel the excitement that would rush through my veins and light the fire in me. The girls get out of the car and stand by the flag pole towards the center of the track. I countdown from five with my hand and let it drop outside the window at one so they know it's time for me to push the gas to the limit. The roar of the engine doesn't awaken anything inside me, but as I go around the second turn I smile a shit eating grin. I feel Atlanta's presence next to me. I know she isn't there in the physical sense but her soul is next to me cheering me on. The white dice hanging from the rear view mirror are so still even though the wind is blowing through the windows. It's her. She's here.

After the third turn I push the gas further than I have before. I continue driving hard until I have finished three laps. I put the car in park and the girls run down to the track. Camry runs up to me and plows into my arms and wraps hers around my neck. I place my hands on her hips and give her a slight push back.

"That was an awesome run." Dani bursts.

"I can't tell you how good it felt to push this beauty to the limit." I slap my hand on the hood of the car. "It was like riding a bike."

Camry is still as giddy as a teenage girl. "Can I drive it?"

"Have you driven on a track before?" I question.

"No but I'd love to try it." She claps her hands together and gives me a begging look.

I have to admit it's a cute face but I'm not in the position to handle another accident. "How about we practice on the straightway first. It's not as easy as it looks with the car at the speed you need it to be. I need to see how you drive. You can drive me around in your car one day so I can get a feel of how comfortable you are in it."

She nods, "Okay but I'd love to do it soon."

I shrug my shoulders, "I guess."

I'm not too thrilled about another lady in my life being around the racing scene. Heck, I'm not even sure this is a life I want anymore.

Racing has always been in my veins, but I feel a blockage now preventing me from moving forward. It's quite possible I will never be at the final step of grieving because I won't let go of Atlanta. It's only been a few months, but it feels like it is happening on this very instant. The pain is so strong that before I climb out of my bed in the morning I take in a deep breath, close my eyes and say aloud, *Atlanta be with me today so I can feel you around me*. I walked away from the stairs, but my heart never walked away from the love I have for her. The way I miss just knowing she was alive and a phone call away. It was enough to motivate me to walk, to breathe. Every day that passes is another day I am living a lie.

Ed, my parents, Atlanta's family and Dani have spent every day since trying to get me to be okay. I have heard them talk about ideas of bringing me comfort so I can move on, but I see Atlanta in all of them. It's so painful, but I go through the motions of my everyday life, smile and pretend I am getting better however when the doors are closed and the lights are out I am still waiting for her to return to the land of the living.

I tell the girls it's getting late and I should take them home.

"Camry, would you like to stay with me tonight since it's so late? I can take you to your car in the morning." Dani chimes in, noticing my solemn tone.

One thing about Dani is that she has known me so long she can tell when I need to be alone.

"Yeah, a sleepover would be awesome. I haven't done that since I was in grade school." Camry giggles, wrapping her arm between Dani's.

I can tell she is super thrilled about the girl bonding by the slight roll of her eyes. We all hop in the car and after locking up I take the girls to Dani's car at the gallery. She lives a block away so it is much closer than Camry's house on the outside of town.

I drive around for a couple hours. Nowhere to go but home, yet that was the last place I wanted to be. I wanted so bad to drive down to the park and demand the stairs to appear. I wanted her to grab ahold of my hand and lead me to the top. I'm foolish for even thinking it was possible or that our path was meant for us to be together in the end, but I held on and no matter how difficult it has been I've stayed away until now.

I turn the car around and drive straight to the park. The street lights are bright and have the park lit up just enough that you can see through the soft mist of fog beginning to form in the air. I am alone at this late hour at night, which is good since I don't feel like having people stare at me. The more I walk down the path the more the fog comes into view and the teal blue pinwheels line the sidewalk until I reach the bottom of the staircase. I glance around and tonight the pinwheels have filled the lawn of the park for as far as the eye can see. The fog is stronger but with the street lamps bring a tranquil appearance and I can't help but to keep gazing at every inch of it.

My eyes flicker to the stairwell and I notice that it is still. No angel coming down the steps to bring me the feeling I have been longing for since the last time I was here. I sit at the bottom step and I wait but she never shows. I'm empty.

Months ago I left here with the knowledge I wouldn't come back and I would do everything I could to move on but with every passing day I find my body aching for her voice, her touch, to see her face but I am left with nothing. She set me free and I've lost her forever this time.

I stand and face the monster size staircase that fades through the fog. It doesn't feel like the times before when I could feel her presence or even when I was driving the car earlier and I felt her there. This time I feel nothing. Why is she doing this to me and making me suffer out here like this? Doesn't she know the pain I am in without her?

I cop a squat on the cold damp sidewalk in front of the staircase and wait. I wait until I can no longer hold my eyes open from the exhaustion that floods my body and takes over my brain. My weak eyes close and I drift off to sleep on the cold wet ground. I am awakened by the noise of the city coming alive around me. I sit up and try to get my barring. Once I realize I spent the entire night on the ground asleep waiting for Atlanta to show up, I pick myself off the ground and stride back to my car.

I call in sick to work. Ed assured me there was no work that was in dire need of completion which helped with the guilt I felt for lying. He doesn't deserve the white lie, but I can't handle the pressure of living today. I go to my apartment and lock the door behind me. I walk over to the kitchen cabinet, open it and pull out one of Atlanta's favorite coffee mugs with Zombie Cure wrote along the side of it. I sit in on the countertop and start a pot of coffee. Once it is ready, I pour it into the cup and pad into the living room and take a seat on the couch. The hot drink slides down my throat and burns as I take in a swig.

I sit in silence and glance around the room. I bring up every memory I can fathom and I still ache for more. After a lifetime with your soulmate, your best friend and lover I don't see what is left. I've lived and I've died without ever leaving this earth, never walking the stairs to a better place. I'm dead and stuck here in this hell. This is hell. You never hear of anyone waking up from a coma and saying, "I saw the fire". It's always how they've seen the light. Their loved ones on the other side. You know why? Because we are already in the fire. We are trapped here in hell while all our loved ones move on the heaven. Half of us fear death because we don't know what will be in store for us, but if they knew there was only one place left to go, and it was a perfect place then maybe they would let go of the stress of day to day life and let death take them sooner instead of waiting for an accident, illness or a lunatic to take them there.

I fear life because I know how beautiful heaven is from Atlanta's face to the massive wings that she now is wearing. How can they expect to show me all that is good and leave me here as if my vision of heaven and death hasn't changed? One simply does not move on from the stairs.

27

Holding on to hope

     I drive down to the park and walk to the bench near the water bank. It's been months and no sign of movement on the stairs. It's like she moved on from me, yet I know the truth is that she believes not seeing me will help me move on. I'm pissed, because she said she would be here until I no longer needed her; but where is she? Exactly, she is up there and I'm here alone. Doesn't she get that no matter how much time passes, she will always be the woman I will ever need in my existence. I don't have a desire to love anyone else or to even halfway bring another person into my life. No one could compare to the perfect woman I've loved all my years on this earth. It's not about an attractive woman, physically fit, beautiful face or even a kind heart of any other lady except my soulmate. The human that was taken from me too soon and left an enormous hole in my heart which will never be filled with anyone else. I've tried. I dated several ladies that were in most ways almost perfect, yet they would never be perfect. There was only one person or now a ghost that was capable of that. Atlanta.

     I scream out, "Come down just one more time."

     A couple and their two kids stop walking and stare over at me. The mother pulls her kids closer like she is shielding a deranged lunatic from them. I wave and stay quiet the remainder of my time there.

I will never understand how someone can call a person their soulmate and still look for another to replace them. Your soulmate makes you whole, healed, and complete, like there is a piece of the puzzle missing from your life. I think a majority of the human population confuses a soulmate with a life partner. A life partner is someone you have a deep friendship with that makes you feel secure, whole.

A soulmate and you have a connection beyond interests and it feels like you can't breathe when they aren't near you, but somehow you feel them and begin breathing until they return. Your soulmate doesn't have to be in the same place as you to know what you are feeling, and for them to feel it too. That's the connection Atlanta and I shared. We felt each other's emotions without ever speaking a word or reacting without facial expressions.

She is playing hard ball with me by keeping her distance. I can sense that it is what she thinks is best and if the tables were turned, I would do the same thing except the fact that I am selfish in ways that she isn't. I would want to be near her even if I knew that the best thing I could do for her is to let her go. Set free the one you love…yeah that's a joke. Who does that crap? Her I suppose. I could never be that selfless, but she was always an angel even on earth. Under all those tattoos was a pure soul. Well, if you exclude that time she stole that bag of chips from the convenience store when Tommy Northrop dared her to in the eighth grade.

It will never matter how much time has passed. I will never give up on her. Not even an ounce of my heart will stop trying to get her to stroll down those stairs back to me, and not a day will go by that I won't stop here and pray for her to return to me.

I know she can't take me with her, but damn it maybe she will have enough of seeing my sad, sappy body stepping all over the pinwheels that line the way to her that she will put in a good word for me and have me get caught in a gun fire or something. I twist my lips, yeah right. I'm not that lucky.

28
Year of Hell

It's been a year since they pulled the plug on Atlanta and her heart stopped beating. I have spent my days working and evenings looking for a way to drown out the ache that fills me. Tonight is the anniversary of her accident and I'm ready to forget. Camry and I have been hooking up off and on this past year. We help each other with the loss we have experienced but it's just a warm body for a short amount of time. No real healing.

"How's it going?" I ask Camry as I sit next to her at the bar.

"Same shit. Different day. How was work this week? What's the car of the week?" She rubs her index finger down the sweat on the glass in front of her.

I hold my hand up letting the blonde bartender know I am ready to order. "Belair, The basic classic upgrades and style."

"I'm on my third drink, so it looks like you will be driving tonight." She informs me and I take in a deep breath.

I wanted to forget today by drinking the thoughts away but looks like she had other plans. One year ago I lost my best friend and soulmate. Today I have not moved on but at the same time I try to let it go so I can live. That's where the nights of drinking come in. It's my idea of living since for a few meaningless hours I don't feel anything. I don't think about her or the life we are missing out on. Instead, I attempt to dance, sing karaoke with Camry and sometimes we hang out with Dani.

After a few drinks for me, and I've counted a total of six for Camry we end up on the dance floor. Our bodies sway to the beat of the music.

Her arm draped over my shoulder and her head lays on my chest. It's a fast song but something in the drunk state she is in has her in a mellow mood. She isn't the average stand on the table dancing chick when she's drunk. She's mellow and solemn. I think her personality is a lot like mine, but most nights the wild slutty type woman is what I need. It helps pass the time. Camry is the type of girl you date and marry. I'm looking for a one night fling that holds no feelings in me or for me.

"Hey girl. I should drive you home now. It's late and I'm really tired from the long day I've had." I explain, grasping her hand and walking to the bar to grab her jacket off the stool.

She giggles. "Okay but I want you to sleep over."

She stumbles into my side as we walk to my truck. "I think I can manage that." I open the truck door and help her inside. She falls back slightly as she shoots in the passenger seat.

My arm reflux naturally clasps her butt as I push her the rest of the way inside. "Whoa there mister. We will be at my house before you know it. I'm not a back seat kind of gal." Her eyes intensify.

"If I wanted, I'm sure I could convince you but I won't on the pure fact that you are a little intoxicated." I grin and shut the door before walking to the driver's side and getting in.

I crank the truck and back out of the space and begin the short drive to Camry's house. I glance over at her in the passenger seat. Her head is wobbling back and forth from the alcohol. I let out a small chuckle watching her try and keep her eyes open. "I'll wake you once we get there if you want."

Her sleepy eyes peer over at me and her words slur, "I'm… I'm okay. I just don't want to be alone anymore. Dare, do you think you will ever love again?"

It's not the first time she has asked me that and I'm certain it won't be the last. I used to answer no but today I just want to move on and if I say yes then maybe, just maybe my heart can be free and I can find love again; with Camry even. "Yes." The word slips out before I can stop it. Her once wobbly head straightens and her sleepy eyes enlarge as she stares silently out the windshield. Two or four minutes pass by before she says anything. "You will." She questions surprised then her voice softens.

"She would want that for you. Everyone needs love to survive this world. Even after you've had the best and felt the soul of another." Camry slides over in the middle of the seat placing her hand on my leg. "You can't hold on forever, Dare. You deserve to live too."

I know she's right. It's been a year and I still go to the park and wait for her. A damn ghost. She's gone and I'm here living a dead man's life. Today is a new beginning. When I drop Camry off at her house, I take her inside and help her to her bed. I remove her shoes and place them on the floor next to her dresser. When I stand up and turn toward her, I notice the artwork on her walls. It's Atlanta and me. *She was the high bidder.* She has had the originals displayed in her room all this time. Why hasn't anyone told me it was her? Not Dani and not her.

"You...you were the high bidder the night of Dani's gallery opening?" I glare down at her in the bed.

In her drunken state, her eyes soften and she responds quietly, "I just... saw the love between you both and I wanted to be surrounded by it. My life has never had that kind of true love in it. Not from my parents and not my personal life. It was perfect. I just wanted something to remind me that love is possible."

"I need to take a step back from you. Not because you bought the art but because I need to heal myself before settling down so quickly. You were the first girl that I have allowed myself to be with since Atlanta. Camry, you deserve more than I can give you right now. You deserve perfect and you deserve a soulmate. I've already found mine and I won't have another one." She is sad when I tell her my decision, but at the same time she agrees.

"I don't want to keep my hopes up when you've never given me a reason to until tonight. We are both broken and we both need to see what else is out there before we will ever know if we truly have feelings for one another or if we are the security blanket we can't leave home without." She peers over at me. Her eyes are glistening from the built up tears in them.

"I don't want to be a security blanket and you shouldn't either. We should have passion and bring out the happiness in each other. Instead I feel like all we do is remind each other of the pain. It's not healthy." Grabbing her hand I take it in mine and place my other one on top of it. "Let's just see what else is there in case we are blankets and we are holding ourselves back from something else."

She lets out a small sob. "Okay. Will we still talk?"

"All the time. Friends no matter what." I lean in and wrap my arms around her.

Dani and I meet up at the coffee shop next to her gallery so she can tell me some exciting news. I haven't seen her in a couple weeks but we text daily. I have no clue what it could be so once we order our coffee I began quizzing her down.

"Spill the news." I demand as I grab her coffee from the barista and had it to her.

"So, I met someone and I would like you to meet him." She grabs the coffee out of my hands and tucks her lavender strands behind her ear.

"Wow. You didn't text me anything about a guy. What's with all the hush hush?" I grab my coffee from the barista and we walk outside to a small table with a black umbrella for shade in the middle.

"It's not hush. More like I didn't want to jinx myself with this guy. His name is Nick Scottsman. We met at the gallery a couple weeks ago when he purchased a painting for his mom as a birthday gift. I was smitten from that moment on. He's great but I need another opinion in case I'm blinded and I don't want to end up with a dud. I'm too old to stay single for much longer." She laughs.

Her entire face lights up as she explains how they met and it's enduring. It's been too long since I've recognized something other than sadness in anyone. Atlanta would be so overjoyed by the news and I know she is probably a big part of Nick coming into Dani's life.

"So when would you like me to meet him? Any special event planned or maybe just a quiet dinner?" I push up my flannel sleeve toward my elbow and hen the other side. "I could scare him a little. Threaten him like a big brother."

She wraps her arms around her stomach and laughs, "I don't think you need to go overboard. Maybe just some drinks at Mouth. There is a heart disease event this weekend. Are you game?"

I ponder for a second about stepping in that bar but quickly the feeling is shaken and I agree. "Sounds like a date or meet a date night."

We finish our coffee, hug and then we both go our separate ways. The week is halfway over and I am already pumped up for the weekend. Meeting Nick will be nice change of pace and maybe I'll meet a nice girl at the event. Someone caring and without drama or sadness.

I make it to the garage and notice the Bel Air is rolled out of the shop and a dusty as a fireplace mantel after years of not being cleaned.

"What happened?" Throwing my hands up in the air, my voice reaches a new vocal height from nearly running once I got out of my truck.

Ed begins laughing hysterically. "Well the vacuum was switched from suck to blow and this is the result. By the time I realized what was happening it was so dusty that I had to get the boys to help me push the car out as well ourselves, so we could let the dust settle. They are in there cleaning it up."

"At least it was something simple. It looked like a bomb went off or something when I pulled up here." I chuckle and slide my finger over the hood of the car. "I'll take this to the back for a wash. You should go clean off too."

"Will do." Ed tosses me the keys and strolls into the office.

A part of me wants to wash this car and go work on it but I decide that now is a good time to take the rest of the day off. I finish cleaning the car, pull it into the clean garage and stroll into the office. "Hey Ed. I'm going to take the rest of the day off if that's okay. I feel like I'm getting a cold."

He nods. "Sure thing. Now don't be laying around playing video games. Get some rest boy."

"You got it." I mummer before turning on my heels and make my way to my truck.

I'm not sick. I'm well, single. It's time for me to spend some time with as many opposite sex as I can find. With Camry and Atlanta out of the picture I need to experience the life most men my age are living. Late nights, alcohol and women. Lots of women. I drive home and shower. I pick up my phone off the kitchen counter and text Steven.

Me: what's your night look like? I need a wing man.

Steven: I was going to change the oil in my truck but I'd rather take turns playing wing man with you.

Me: Meet me at my house in an hour?

Steven: 10/4

I was damn lucky that he was free and all too willing to go on the town with me. The bully who turned into a best bud has always had my back and I, his. He spent years trying to dare me to tell Atlanta my feelings for her and when I chickened out he always kept my secret. Spending most of our time together telling me how stupid I was for not fessing up. He was right. I wasted time being scared. Life is too short to let fear write your story.

Steven came walking through the door of Atlanta's apartment like he lived here. "Hey man. Bad day?"

"I am ready to put myself back out there and see where the night takes me." I grab my keys off the table and walk to the door, opening it and directing him out.

"I know it's been rough but this is the best thing for you." Steven clasps his hand on my shoulder before walking down the stairs to my truck.

"Still driving this ragged ole thing?" He asked before opening the door and climbing in the front seat.

"Yeah. It does the job." I murmur as I turn the keys in the ignition and the truck engine roars. It still sounds just as sexy as the day my parents bought it for me.

The first bar of the night was a bust so we drove downtown for some more action at the Cowboy Buck Up Bar. Steven quickly hooked up with a brunette that pulled him on the dance floor for grinding and make out sessions like most of the crowd here. I sat at the bar and ordered a beer on tap. The bartender was a cute blonde with an amazing smile and every time she would catch me looking in her direction she would let out a faint giggle. I couldn't help but notice her since she was stunning and she knew it.

When she came back toward me, I inched my finger at her so she would lean in to me. "What's your name?" I asked.

She leaned in a little closer almost touching my earlobe, "Name is Jessie, love. I don't recall seeing you in here before."

"It's been a while since I've came in. Maybe sometime last year. When did you start?"

She brushes her hand on my arm, "Oh, I started three months ago. I started as a waitress, and I've been bartending for a couple weeks now."

"What time do you get off?"

"Closing tonight." She leans back and makes a mixed drink for one of the ladies at the bar that ordered it. Glimpsing over at me she calls out, "Wanna hang out afterward?"

"Yeah. Looks like my buddy has a way home tonight." I nod toward Steven on the dance floor.

We spend the next hour making fun of the drunks that come up to the bar. I've had a few but some of the folks, mainly girls are so wasted that their words slur when ordering. This barely legal brunette nearly lands in my lap when she slips off the barstool beside me.

'Hey girl, are you okay?' I ask as I help her up from my leg. Her head wobbles and her eyes are glassy like ice. I'm not sure she should even have another drink at this point and it makes me wonder if the bartender actually cuts people off when they can tell they've had too much to drink. From the looks of it, they don't.

The young girl has a sly smile stretch across her face before her slurring words flood from her mouth, "You wanna dance?"

"No thanks sugar. I think you have had a bit much to drink and I like my women coherent." Standing, I flatten my jeans out with my palms and lean in toward Jessie.

"I will see you outside when you get off." She nods and I proceed to make my way outside stopping only for a second to tell Steven. I would talk with him tomorrow. He is way too wrapped up in the chick he is with to even care about where I am going.

Thirty minutes pass by before Jessie joins me outside. We hop in my truck that I have pulled out front of the car and I drive to my house. Not Atlanta's place but mine. I'd never take a girl there. That was her place. Ours.

Jessie switches the radio station to a country channel and begins bouncing around in the seat to one of the new songs that has hit top of the billboard charts. I'm not one for music these days but the song is pretty good. I picture for a half a second Atlanta singing it and as good as it felt to think of her I shook it off and focused on the girl waving her hands in the air. I was beginning to think she took a few shots of what she was pouring at the bar due to her over eagerness to act like the usual bar hopping socially needy girls.

I have been searching for something since I lost the love of my life and this is what I get. A girl with no real substance. I don't know why it bothers me when the fact is we both know that tonight is a one night deal. I'm not a permanent catch. I'm a horny man that is trying to find some way to live this meaningless life until my existence is no longer an issue. I pull into my driveway and stop the truck at the back door of the trailer.

"Dude, your place is so cute. Do you have roommates?" She jumps out of the passenger door and waits for me by the steps.

Walking to the door I pull my keys out and open it. "No, it's just me."

"Good, I'd hate to have to be quiet." The words come out like a tease but all I hear is 'I'm a slut' and for tonight that's all I need.

Jessie spends most of the night auditioning for the Olympics I think or quite possibly trying a new form of yoga. Granted I enjoyed being the student. The girl had moves. I called her a cab so I didn't have to leave the house and she wasn't about to stay at my house all night. I'd be waking up with a broken bone and I'm not talking skeletal either.

The next few months I go on like this. One chick after another. Sex was the only thing that other women had that I wanted. I used one after another and went about my life as if I wasn't doing anything wrong. Not one care of anyone other than myself and my needs. The need to find something I was missing became so great that I began going out every night and hooking up with another girl. After spending the night having my way with them I would send them home without a contact number until I meet Julie.

30
Unoccupied Mind

Julie was different from the recent women I have been around. She was graceful and very well put together. She was sitting at a table around the edge of the dance floor the first time I laid eyes on her. She swayed with the music but it didn't matter how hard her friends tried, she would not get up and dance. Some of her friends even topped her legs and gave her a lap dance. Her expression was so damn cute that I couldn't help but chuckle. I caught myself feeling emotions that I haven't felt in a long while. Sweaty palms and a fast beating heart. It was just the kick in the ass I needed to get up and talk to her.

I strolled smoothly over to her table and slid a beer toward her. "Here, I think you need another one after your friend pried herself from your leg."

Her cat like eyes glared at me with annoyance. "Thanks but no thanks."

Her words cut through my chest like a dagger. I pushed my chest with my hand and gasped for air. Just like every scorned man would do in this situation. "Girl that hurt. Deep. Deep inside. Seriously though, I just wanted to get you another drink after what looked like a good time. Free of charge and nothing expected." I walked away from her table. Slowly thinking she would change her mind, but as my luck would have it, she didn't take the bait.

I swing my head around and jokingly throw out another option, "You could buy me one if you'd prefer."

Somehow that made her lips perk up into the cutest damn grin. I turn and make my way back to her table. "Have a seat mister. What's your name?" She points at the chair in front of her.

"Hi, I'm Dare." My heart pumps a little harder as I get my name out. I know it's crazy, but it's like my first date even though I've been on a lot lately. They weren't like this though. Taking a girl to your bed is a lot easier than holding a conversation with her. Lots of girls these days have no respect for themselves and go home with any one. The ones that you have to work to get in bed…now those you keep.

"Well, hey Dare. I'm Julie. My friends drug me here to get over my resent break up. I'm not sure if they were hoping I'd drink him away or whore him away. They have good intentions but I'm more of a sulk and brut kind of girl." Her eyes flash up at me and I see the playfulness in them. She picks the glass up in her hand and raises it to her full lips, drinking the last of it. After she sits the empty bottle down she slides the one I bought closer to her and wraps both hands around it.

"A recent break-up huh. I am all too familiar on that. Men, and I'm not including me in that category but men tend to make mistakes when it comes to the women in their lives. I would almost bet he is already regretting it."

Not sure what to say, I ramble off some crazy words that flow out like non-stop rain into a bucket. *Oh please shut up, Dare.*

"Well, it don't matter much. I'm better off alone than with a man that don't see my worth, while he is with me. Life is too short to wait around for someone to figure it out." She places her index finger on her bottom lip pausing before she continues, "What's your story? Looking for a one night stand or are you another douchebag that don't know what he wants." She is blunt.

"Honest?" I question her.

"If you can be?" She takes a sip of her beer.

"The love of my life died a couple years ago and I am trying to move on. Until I saw you, I had several one night stands. Something about you peaked my interest from across the room and I knew I had to know you more. You seem different." I stop and watch her reaction. Surely, the love of my life line didn't win her over since she is looking for someone that knows what they want, but hell I'm just being honest.

She ponders for a moment, "That's honest. So it's been a couple years and here you are. She must have been amazing. Hard for someone to live up to that kind of love. What makes you think you are even worth someone trying to?"

"I don't expect anyone to live up to her. I just want someone that can live up to them self. Someone I can laugh and enjoy the hell out of what is left of our lives. I'm not asking for much, just happiness." I lean back slightly, but not enough to become unbalanced on the stool.

"Okay, so let's just say for the sake of broken hearts that we do go on a date. Where would we go? I want to see if this is even worth it." Her lips turn up into a half smile and her eyes glisten.

I love how playful she is. I could scoop her in my arms now and take her home but I know that she would probably end up slapping me, and I'm not wanting that kind of reaction from her. "Well, huh. I am not good at being put on the spot like this. Dinner of course, I'd meet you there so you aren't stuck waiting for a ride or for me to take you home if you can't stand me." I chuckle. "Then I think we could go play arcade games and get some ice cream afterwards. Then, we will end at your car or mine, if you'd rather drive so you could leave me at any point of the evening."

She laughs the goofiest laugh the entire time I am telling her our date night plans. "So, I look like an arcade game kind of girl?"

"Not really but I can see deep inside you. It's there, you just hide it from other people. Thanks for letting me in though. I like that part of you." I joke but know that it is the truth. She holds her fun side in and I am the one to release it.

"Okay, so I'm in. When is this date taking place?" She waits for the answer.

"Tomorrow, next week, nah…Now." I exclaim, standing from my stool and offering my hand to her to help her up.

"I thought you said I would meet you at the place for dinner? I don't have my car tonight." She is hesitant on giving me her hand.

"I lied. I'll take you to dinner. There is a diner around the next block and then an all-night arcade a few blocks from here. You ready?" I push my hand out to her again, and this time she takes it.

"Oh wait. I have to tell my friends." She releases my hand and fast paces to her friends that are grinding on some lucky guy. I notice some surprised faces, and one glanced over at me and nudged her in the shoulder with a wink.

When she makes it back over to me, I feel relief wash over me. I was so glad that they didn't convince her she was crazy and make her stay with them. I needed to see how this would play out. She was different and I wanted something that would leave me off guard and wanting more. Julie, did just that. The night was perfect. She was perfect.

We spent the next three months in pure bliss. Dating was something I didn't know all too well since Atlanta and I were friends and the other women were merely obstacles that kept me from my goal. It's sad to say but even dating the perfect girl, I always thought of Atlanta. I couldn't help but compare them. I know that they would never be the same but after your soul has touched its mate, I don't think there is any way your soul could be one-hundred percent complete without the other half.

My soul was still empty. Julie filled the void with her presence but she never completed me.

I am always missing something that I wouldn't get back with her. I hated what I was doing to Julie. Using her like the other men in her life, and being the person I didn't want to be for her. She knew how I felt. We talked about Atlanta and I could see the sadness in her eyes when she realized she would never live up to her. I didn't expect her to, but a part of me expected the pain to go away so that I could move on. Days getting easier like they say would, but they never did. Every day was a struggle to breathe. It's just that some days I would start the day not being able to breathe, and others would end that way.

What is there when your world is gone?

What type of life do you live?

Why bother when you can end things and just be happy in the clouds?

31

Lonely heartbeats

Three years have passed and today marks the anniversary of Atlanta's death. I visit the park every night that I can and pray that she will saunter down the stairs and smile the most flawless smile I can still picture from all the years before. She never appears, but the stairs are there. I never grasped why she didn't appear any more, but the stairs each time did. I never stopped believing she would come back to me.

Life went on without her for three years and I attempted dating, but no one was ever capable in changing the way I felt about someone that is merely a ghost and only a memory. Camry and I dated for a couple months, but I could never move past the fact that Atlanta didn't want her and me together. We still communicate and get together with Dani and her boyfriend Nick. My parents are traveling the country and only come home every couple months if I'm lucky. I always thought that Atlanta and I would be together in rocking chairs when we were eighty, watching our grandchildren play.

It sucks how life changes without warning. On her birthday, May twenty-ninth every single year I have bought her a gift and sat it on the table next to her bed. This year I added to the collection. I'd leave them at the stairs but they are in a park and invisible to everyone but me.

The gifts would quickly be stolen so it wouldn't make since to take them there. She will never open anything from me again, but I know she is watching me from above and that someday, when I see her again she will be able to tell me what she thought of each one.

Earlier this year Ed retired and entrusted me the garage. I spend most days and nights there working on the beauties that used to bring me so much satisfaction. Now, it's a job that must be done just like every breath I take is another function I have to do on a daily basis. I dream of her every night as I sleep alone in her bed. The emptiness has locked me in, and I find no hope of escaping. The dark hole is filled with quicksand and it won't let me go. I relinquished myself and I'm content with my choice. Life isn't worth living without her.

I spend the day in the record room listening to the music that generated such pleasure for him and her, so much inspiration for her own music. Damon sealed this room off a couple years back, because he couldn't bare anyone obtaining the records that she loved so much. The aroma of incense still saturates the air from in the walls that caught every puff of smoke from the fragrance filled stick unlike her pillow that no longer smells of her, but instead of me. I tried spraying her perfume on it, or the hair spray that she used, but nothing stuck longer than a day or two. I still pick up the bottles and take a whiff just to smell her from time to time, but it's not the same as it once was.

After hours of listening to music alone I decide it's time to pay my respects at her gravestone. I hate visiting the place where her body is buried, because I know where her soul is and her spirit. It's down at the park I visit every day. However, on the anniversary of her death, I still choose to visit the grave where her body is located.

I stop at the local florist and pick up her favorite flowers and three purple balloons, one for every year she has been gone. When I get to the site I set the flowers in the vase next to the headstone and place the balloons on the other side tied to a silver weight to hold them down. Her family hasn't been out here yet from the looks of things, so I pull at the dried up weeds and sweep off the concrete slab with the mini broom from my truck, so it looks nice when her mom visits today. Atlanta would have wanted me to watch over her family since she is unable to do so now. I do make weekly visits to their house and have dinner with them. It's our Wednesday night tradition now. It is hard to be there listening to her dad reminisce about her childhood or hearing the slips her mom makes about how she would like this meal. Sometimes I feel like a constant reminder of the child they lost and think that it might be easier for them if I stayed away, however without missing a beat Mrs. Reed texts me every Wednesday to make sure I will be there for dinner. I will continue to go until the text no longer appears on my phone.

I take a seat on the grass next to the slab and I stare at it for some time. I don't have anything to say to the empty concrete because I know she isn't here, yet here I sit. I don't know if I am waiting for her angel wings to appear or if I am at a loss as to what to say. I'm sure it's a little of both. The last time we spoke I thought we had more time. The last time I held her hand it never crossed my mind that I wouldn't have another chance to fill her flesh on mine. The smoothness of her skin would never again send chills down my spine.

Death should come with a warning or at least something to soften the blow some. Instead, all we got were screams from the fear she had as she watched that bastard drive the car towards her.

The bastard that is still alive and even though he spends his days in a cell, he still breathes the same air as I do. Justice isn't justice when someone deserves to suffer in the most painful of ways. Instead, he will work and watch the television while hard working people like me pay for it, until one day he will die from old age or if I'm lucky someone will take him out when the lights are out. No, I shouldn't have these thoughts, but I do. The anger consumes me as it did three years ago. The same horrible thoughts invade my mind and keep me from being rational. Thankfully, he is nowhere near Nashville and I have no interest in leaving this town until I take my last breath.

"I just wish I could see you one more time, to hear your voice and to feel your skin against mine." I whisper, close my eyes, and push myself up off the ground. When I open my eyes I see her standing face to face with me. I am confused, but relieved she is still here with me. "Atlanta. I've missed you." I reach out and touch her face, my palm clasping her cheek.

"I know. Dare, this is the last time I will be here like this."

"Where are the stairs? Why can't you see me every day like before?" I question.

"You see, the only reason I am here now is to bring you home with me."

I am puzzled. What does she mean bring me with her? I can't go with her, but…I want too.

"You lost me. What are you talking about?" I gaze into her sparkling eyes looking for answers.

She tugs at my arm and pulls me a few steps away from the gravesite. "Turn around."

I do as I am told and I am shocked when I notice my body is laying on the ground next to the slab. I twist back towards her. "Am I dead?"

"Yes." She whispers and clasps my hand with a tight grip. She is quiet as I let the words sink in.

"How did I die? I was just here talking to you or the stone." I glance back at my body and choke on the words.

"Dare, you had a blood clot and it reached your heart. I'm sorry." She informs me and I know I should be sad or angry, but I am relieved. I have been waiting so long to join her and here I am standing next to her and touching her skin. There is no other place I'd rather be. No, death isn't the answer, but when you are no longer living and the universe decides this is the answer you accept it and move on. This was my fate. This isn't the end but a new beginning. I look back at my body once more and then back to Atlanta, "Let's go home."

32

Souls as One

Atlanta and I climb the stairs together for the last time. Our souls are connected in ways we will never be able to explain, but whatever the reason we were brought together again so we could continue the relationship we had and live our eternity as one. The past few years have been the worst I could have imagined, but now for whatever reason I am reunited with my love.

I don't look back because there is nothing for me in that world. I squeeze Atlanta's hand and walk further up the stairs. The clouds open up and I see the light that you hear so much about on earth. The bright light is warming to your skin and it sparkles like glitter the closer you are to it. It's rather breathtaking.

Once we reach the top of the staircase she pauses and turns to me. "This is your last chance? You have a choice. You can continue on and join me here, or you can go back to earth and live your life for many more years."

I never thought we had a choice in if we stay or go, but here I am at a crossroad from earth and heaven. The choice for me is simple. "I'll follow you anywhere." I squeeze her hand and take a step into the cloud-filled path. The more we walk the more things open up.

The clouds glide over and become more transparent. We come to a large golden door that is covered in tiny carved artwork. I can't quite make out the images because they are so small but the larger images they create are beautiful. It is a man and woman embracing each other. The love between them is shown in the eyes. I gaze at Atlanta, "Soulmates like us." I murmur.

The door opens slowly and I get to observe what she loves so much about being here. We step through the door and are greeted by two older Angels. The skin shows the age, but it glows so perfect that you don't notice it as an imperfection. "Welcome to heaven, Dare. We heard that you couldn't live with your entire heart on top of these clouds." The old woman utters.

"You heard right." I smiled back at her.

I shift my eyes to my surroundings. I observe every inch. The ground is clouds and the walkway is clear, but somehow I know I can walk on it without falling through. Angels are flying all around us, however some are walking. They seem to be like humans in every way except the flying and wings. Wait, no, their beauty here is unmistakable.

"Do you have a house? Silly question huh?" I question Atlanta.

She tells the older couple we will see them later and she tugs me to follow her. "We don't have houses like on earth, however there are areas that are for us. Come and I will show you."

We continue to stroll down the transparent path until we reach what appears to be an elevator. It's clear as well, but I can make it out. The door opens and we step inside. Atlanta pushes the button and then in an instant the door closes and reopens. I don't even think it moved yet we are in a different area.

"Everything here is magic. If you want it then it will happen. There are rules you must follow, but they are simple and you will know them without anyone explaining them. You see angels are good. No one here likes to break a rule." She strides inside the room. "This is our space."

I take a look around. It's a small space with a white couch and a circle table with an overly large glass ball on top.

"It's a view to earth. We can watch our friends and family and from time to time we can send tiny symbols to let them know we are watching. A dream, an object, a song, just something small, but they know and they always smile." Atlanta brings me over toward the table.

My parents are in the magical orb. I feel sad for them, but I am also so content to be here with Atlanta that I know I am where I should be. Something about this place gives me a sense of completion and joy. Who knew death could be so beautiful?

Humans only see the pain and sorrow that fill their hearts after they have lost a loved one but one day when it's their turn to walk the stairs to Heaven they will understand why we are taken and what is beyond the golden gate. It's peaceful and perfect with your entire world laid at your feet.

"Now I understand all the times you told me you were happy. It wasn't because you were happy without me, but instead because you were literally in heaven." I murmur glancing in the orb.

"I watched you every day. I know the struggles you had to deal with when you lost me. It wasn't easy seeing that. I'm sorry for all the pain you endured. All I wanted was for you to find someone amazing and have cute little Dare babies." Atlanta smiles and grabs my hand. "I love you. I've missed you more than I've missed my Mustang...so you know that's a lot."

"I don't have to ask why Heaven made you happy anymore, because my eyes are wide and clear enough now to know. I do have a question though." I pause, taking in a deep breath before continuing. "Why did you stop coming to see me even when I showed up every day for years?"

"Dare, I had to stop visiting because it wasn't helping you move forward. I knew you needed time, though I didn't know you would never get over me. I knew our love was strong, yet I kept telling myself that not one person could love me so much that they would stop living just to be with me." Atlanta grabs my hand and squeezes it.

"I'll follow you anywhere. Even up the longest flight of stairs in the history of stairs and to a place filled with clouds and Angels. Not even death could keep me from loving or following you."

I lean in toward her face and kiss her with deep passion. Our first embrace since I joined her in the afterlife. This time our kiss lasted for what seemed to be an eternity. There were no places to go or things to do except completely engulf each other. Passion in heaven is like nothing you've ever felt before because it is pure and ravishing. We are one and with our souls together in the clouds of heaven we are fully complete.

"As if stairs could keep us apart. I love you more, Dare." She whispers.

I almost thought my mind was playing tricks on me but I quickly realized that it was the voice of angels calling me. Atlanta grabs my hand in excitement and pulls me to follow her. We reach a small crowd of angels and my stomach does flips flops as I await for them to tell me what they want. A small angel breaks through the crowd and nods toward me.

"You called?" I asked confused as to what he wanted but scared that they changed their mind and I'm going back to earth.

"It's time for you to design your wings." The small angel states and leads Atlanta and me to a medium sized flat cloud. We stand on it and the angel questions, "What would you like your wings to look like?"

My mind searches for something. "I would like them to be large chestnut brown with streaks of purple."

The angel smiles as he reaches his hand out in front of him and slowly pushes it vigorously toward me. It was just like magic and I could feel the wings extend from my back and flare out past my shoulders. A golden frame mirror appears and I take my first look at my new wings. They are rich in color with just the right amount of purple.

The feathers are soft and once I touch them I can see why Atlanta is always petting them. They are too soft not to.

"Dare, they are perfect!" Atlanta walks behind me and admires the bird like wings.

"And so are you." I respond.

"I love you, Atlanta." I breathe in.

"And I love you. To the clouds and back." Atlanta smiles and wraps her arms around my neck.

I place my hand on her cheek, brushing my thumb slowly across her skin, "and up a million stairs, I'll follow you anywhere." I embrace her in a kiss. "Anywhere."

And they lived happily in the hereafter...

The end

Acknowledgements

Thank you God for waking me up to miracles and true love. Thank you for giving me another chance and saving my soul so I can become a better person and daughter to you. You gave me back my faith and life.

I want to thank my dad and sister for all the years that they were in my life. Even though they weren't long enough I know that the stairs will lead me to you someday when it's my turn to join you.

Cassie, my beautiful and talented daughter. I would not have finished this book if it wasn't for you, your support and encouragement over the last two painful years of my life. There will never be enough thank you's, to express how grateful I am for you. My best friend and my person. I will follow you anywhere. Morefinity!

Thank you to my husband for never discouraging me from this author dream.

My three moms, (Ann, Patti and Val) you have all three taught me so many things that helped me grow into this crazy, yet sane person I am today.

Thank you so much to the friends, family and fans that have patiently waited for me to complete this story and finally publish it. Your support amazes me and warms my heart.

Thank you to my editor Mary Ann Jock for putting up with 2 years of one chapter edits and too many crazy emails due to my personal life. Your patience with me will not be forgotten.

Thank you to my Beta readers. Laura, Leeah, Chely, Cassie, and Jen- Your opinions and friendship are greatly valued.

About the author

Christy Dilg writes where her heart leads her from erotica to paranormal. She wants her stories to inspire and make her readers think about their own lives; all while adding some sexy characters in the mix.

When Christy isn't writing she enjoys reading, hiking, listening to the oldies and spending time with her family including her two fur babies. Frenchie "Griffin" and Yorkie "Kellan" named after her favorite book. (Can you guess?) Amongst her other addictions are Snapchat, beards, and beer.

Christy has always wanted to be a writer since as long as she can remember and after getting thyroid cancer, she decided that it was now or never.

Social Media

Website: www.christydilg.com

Instagram: @fancy_grey

Snapchat: fancy_grey

Twitter: @fancygrey

Facebook: www.facebook.com/authorchristyadilg

Proof

Made in the USA
Columbia, SC
03 June 2017